Father, Creator, Spirit -
Transform

by

Deborah Lamoreaux

PROLOGUE

Alcindor had an important conversation with the Redeemer, as he sat in solitude and waited for Detective Danielle Almonzo to enter a conference room of the New York City police department's 15th precinct.

Now, he knew exactly what he needed to do.

Was anxious to see it done too, for her to progress on her journey, and so he could return to his customary form.

As he rubbed at the faint pain in his back, he gained a new and very healthy respect for elderly humans. Transforming from an angel into an old man was certainly not without its challenges, but he knew he was now someone she'd be very receptive to, given her past life experience.

"Ah, good morning, Detective." He used his cane to push himself upright as she entered. He dialed his bliss down to a pleasant buzz and extended his right hand across the small table. "Thank you so much for taking the time to meet with me." She shook it, an expression of curiosity crossing her face, even as she smiled. She indicated the seat he'd just vacated with a pointing hand. He retook it and she then sat, opposite him, in one of the other three chairs.

"Certainly, Mr. …?"

"Oh, just call me Al."

"Okay, Al. What can I help you with today? I hear you asked for me by name." She gave him a shrewd look. "Have we met before? You seem familiar to me somehow."

"Oh, you know what they say Detective, I've probably just got one of those faces."

"Yeah…probably."

He could sense her faint confusion, but she let it go.

"Well, truth be told, I'm actually hoping I can help you."

"Oh? How so?"

He leaned in closer and lowered his voice.

"What would you say if I told you that our Verndari visitors aren't really what they appear, or claim to be?"

"I'd say…tell me more." In contrast to him, she rocked back in her chair, away from the table, but opened her hands for just a moment in a brief gesture of acceptance and interest.

He took it as a good sign and launched right in.

"Well, I've had occasion to get acquainted with one of them." He chose his words carefully. "He's different though. Doesn't align with them or follow their…agenda. From what I've seen, he's got mankind's best interest at heart. He has a plan to open the public's eyes to the truth, day by day, and to ultimately set things right. And–" he shrugged, "– given the right circumstances, I imagine he'd be open to sharing some…of what he knows, with a well-placed ally."

"And what exactly *does* he know?" She placed her elbows on the arms of the chair, leaned forward a bit, and clasped her hands together in front of her face.

"Oh, I'll let him be the one to share that with you, in *His* appointed time. And now that I've spoken with you, and see that you're receptive?" He waited…

Nothing.

"Intrigued then?" He got a single nod of agreement this time. "Good. Then I'll be sure to let him know how he can get in touch with you."

He shifted his hands on the table. Displayed open palms. Inclining his head, he focused his gaze until he held hers, one second…two.

"I've spent a whole lot of time on this planet, and I've seen things that you would struggle to believe Detective. These…aliens…they have a world domination agenda, and I won't say how I know, but not a one of them will rest until all of mankind meets them at the very gates of hell."

She took in a sharp breath, her eyes widening in alarm.

"Trouble is, most people can't see them for the deceivers they are. Their trickery is beguiling, shrouded, and all wrapped up in an enticing, mysterious trap. But underneath it all, trust me, they're the single most devastating threat humanity has ever, or will ever face.

"It's just too bad, it's not real clear and obvious. You know…like a shooting star…"

He watched her eyebrows raise. Her eyes open, as her gaze closely followed his hand making a sweeping arch in the space above and between their heads.

"Across the dark night sky," she finished his thought.

"Exactly."

And just like that…she's on board…

She leaned forward, mirrored his position as she placed her forearms on the table, her hands almost touching his. "You know it's funny you should say all that, because I saw something that made me doubt their intentions as well. Around five years ago. Then…I think because of *them*…something really bad happened–"

"Something that made you lose faith."

Her gaze snapped up to his. Her eyes filled with sudden moisture that she quickly blinked away.

"Yeah…uh…I guess."

He sensed the change in her, even before she withdrew. A retreat that was both physical and mental, into her customary shell. A shell that had done next to nothing to dull the awful pain he knew she'd been living with and successfully hiding, for the past five years.

He felt a swell of pity, yet still tempered by the knowledge of the joy that awaited in her future.

Similar to the key life lesson he'd just imparted as guardian angel to his charge on earth, Alrissa Cole, Detective Danielle Almonzo was also on the cusp of a life altering discovery.

It was all up to her now…

"Well, I'd best be on my way. I've taken up enough of your time." He rose from his seat with the assistance of his cane.

"Yes, and thank you for coming in. I look forward to meeting with your associate in due time." The mask she showed the world was firmly back in place.

He got set to put a crack in it.

He shook the hand she extended, turned, and then slowly headed to the door.

"You know, someone once said, 'Faith is not belief without proof, but trust, without reservation'–" he glanced back at her as he reached the door, and waved a hand over the sensor to open it, "–and that's the thing about faith, Detective, just *trust* you can regain it, and it *will* return. Just as fast as you lost it, and in my experience, much stronger and in a more transformational way than ever before."

"Wait!" The urgency in her tone had him halting in the open doorway.

"How can I get in touch with you again, ah…if I need to."

"Oh, I'm always around." He graced her with his warmest and most reassuring smile. Shared the best blessing he could, across the time and space separating them.

Take heart, dearest child of God…

Dani smiled in return.

What a darling little old guy. So much like her dad, she thought, as a sudden feeling of peace and joy she hadn't felt in years crept in slowly and settled in her heart.

Chapter 1

Psalms 37:32
The wicked watcheth the righteous, and seeketh to slay
him...

JAN 22ND 2120 – NEW ATLANTIS

Dani was right there.

In New Atlantis.

The day chaos erupted all around the city.

Making her way through throngs of panicked pedestrians to get back to her squad car, she stumbled now and then as the tremors beneath her feet grew, along with her anxiety.

Another explosion, so loud this time she dropped to a squat and reflexively covered her head with her hands. She looked up, as she fully expected to see the luminescent dome shatter into a billion pieces and rain debris and then half of the Atlantic down upon her head. Instead, she took a calming breath and watched a cluster of sky ambulances and hover cars whizz by across the bright, artificial sky, high overhead.

Grateful that the dome and the energy shield beyond it seemed to have retained their structure; she rose again and touched the com on her belt. "Dispatch, this is unit 29. We've got a code red. I repeat. A code red!" She looked around, tried to catch her breath as her heart pounded in her ears and out of her chest. "I'm in dome nine, near the northeastern quadrant of sector seven's shield generating plant! Send more units! Hurry!"

"Ten-four officer Almonzo, dispatching two additional units to your location."

"What?!" She looked down at the tiny silver gadget on her belt. Wondered if it was malfunctioning. "Did yuh just completely miss the part where I said this is a code red! Two units? SEND. EVERYONE... NOW, dammit!"

Dumb-ass AI...

She tapped the com to shut it off and started to run.

"All that money spent on a system, and it's not even worth a bad-devil-damn in an emergency," she mumbled under her breath.

"Hey! You people over there!" She skidded to a stop and shouted across the street as she noticed a small group of looky-loos filming the unfolding disaster, instead of fleeing for safety like everyone else, with half a brain.

"Please, head to the evacuation zone in an orderly fashion, for your own safety!" She pointed in the intended direction as she automatically issued the required directive. One of them glanced over and then went right back to angling his wrist cam left and right, intent on capturing the unfolding scene.

"Hey! Are yuh deaf! I just said you people need to get to the evacuation zone! All of you! NOW!"

She ended on a roar, and then held up her badge as a few more of them turned to look at her.

"Sure, officer!" The one who first turned, lifted a hand in her general direction, then raised the index finger on that hand, without even doing her the courtesy of looking at her. "In just one minute."

Aw, hehll no…did he just dis me?

Almonzo resisted the urge to raise a finger of her own, the middle one.

"You know what…?" she mumbled under her breath, "maybe, you can just stay here and die. How about that? Damned if I care. Let the other police units deal with the crowd control.

"And see you on the eleven o'clock news tonight, yuh 'glory-chasing-five-minutes-of-fame-having' morons."

She continued her run.

"Just a routine patrol." Smith had said. "I'll relieve you in an hour or two."

Yeah, right.

"I knew I shouldn't have listened to him and on my day off too. Oh, he better know, payback is a bitch, 'cause he's gonna be in a world of hurt when next I see his sorry butt." She spotted the cruiser where she'd parked it, just a few meters past the corner. She jumped in, threw it in reverse and then sped around the bend. Keeping a sharp eye out, she drove across another two streets going east in the direction of the capital building to see if she could find out what the hell was going on.

And wouldn't you know it, when it rains, it really pours.

She slammed on the breaks.

What now?

A guy. Black hair, big build, and dressed in dark clothing with a backpack on the ground beside him was stooping down a short distance away, just past the entrance to a long, narrow, covered alleyway between two of the sector's power plants. She couldn't be sure, but it looked like he was putting something on the wall of one of the structures.

She put down the passenger side window and shouted. "Hey you! NAPD! Stop whatever it is you're doing and put your hands up where I can see them!"

He froze. Looked in her direction.

"No need officer, I am Verndari!" He called out in a heavily accented voice and resumed his suspicious actions.

"And I...don't give a bad-devil-damn if you're the President of *these* United States!" She climbed out of her car, came around to the pavement in front of the passenger side door, and placed her hand on her firearm. "You better drop whatever it is you're carrying, stand and put your hands up real slow, or you'd best trust and believe, I will put you down!"

He looked back at her and she recognized the expression on his face.

"Don't do it...don't you do it," she said under her breath just as he smirked. He shouldered the backpack as he stood up to his full impressive height, and then started to run, lumbering, given his size, further down the shadowed alley.

"Hey you! Stop!"

A choice expletive escaped her lips.

She ran across the wide pavement and made it

to the wall, just in time to see whatever he placed there just melt into it and disappear. "What in the hell?!" She touched the smooth surface as something beneath the translucent mortar pulsed with an eerie blue light and then was gone.

She looked down the alley and bellowed at the guy's back. "Hey! I said stop! Man, you are gonna be one sorry son of a you-know-what if you make me have to chase after you!"

In my condition…

Grrr… well there was nothing for it. Time to get to work.

She dug deep, took a few quick breaths and started her sprint about fifty meters behind him. Legs and arms pumping, she powered down the alley, so by the time he got to the end of the buildings and rounded the corner, she'd cut the distance between them by half.

Unfortunately for him, he didn't know she'd excelled in track in high school. She grinned. Felt her mood lift, as she enjoyed the expression of surprise that crossed his face as he looked back and noted her progress. He zigzagged into the road. A horn blared loudly as he placed a hand on and then jumped across the hood of a car. Then, as he came right up against a parked one, he lifted the side of it like a toy and pushed it out of his way, up onto the pavement, almost hitting a pedestrian in the process. He looked back over his shoulder and leered, then continued his run, shoving aside anyone he encountered as he went.

"Hey, hey, buddy? You ok?" She bounced on her toes, jogging in place for a moment as she peered at the guy who'd just jumped out of the way of the car. His blue eyes were wide as saucers, his face, pale, and sweating. He gave her a jerky nod, and even though her mind reeled with what she'd just witnessed, she shelved it and kept sprinting.

Along the street she pursued him. He got to the next corner, looked back at her, and went around it. Just before she got there, she saw a bright flash. She slowed and drew her sidearm. Released the safety on the weapon, grasped it with both hands, and then pointed it ahead of her, as she rounded the bend, staying close to the wall.

The teenager who stood before her swung her bag to her back and then slowly held up her hands.

"Sorry, miss." She clicked the safety, lowered the muzzle of the gun, aimed it at the ground. "Did you see a guy in dark colored maintenance overalls come by here just now?"

"Yes. I think so." Her voice sounded strained. Oddly squeaky, and her gaze was directed about a foot above where Dani's head was. Dani glanced back over her shoulder, but there was no one behind her, or any danger that she could see.

"He went that way." The girl pointed across the street.

She had a strange look on her face, and still was not quite meeting Dani's gaze as she gave a slow nod.

"Ok, thanks. Now, go on. Get out of here. And sorry about the gun, I didn't mean to scare you. Just get to the evacuation site as quick as you can. Okay? It's dangerous out here."

Afraid she'd already wasted too much time talking to the girl, she took off running in the direction she'd indicated, but after checking the next block she could find no sign of the defender. She retraced her steps, made it all the way back to the entrance to the alley, to the spot on the wall where she believed she'd seen the strange device. There was absolutely no evidence of it that she could see.

She stepped out of the alley, about to go back to her car when her world tilted. She lost her balance and fell to the pavement beneath her.

Her wrist phone rang just as she braced that hand on a wall, to regain her footing. She looked down, tapped the face.

"Hey babe, gotta call you back. There's been some kind of attack on the domes."

"I know…it's flooding fast. I'm so sorry. Dani."

Icy fear gripped her by the throat.

"Oh, God, Joey, where are you?" Frantic, she tried to get video on the timepiece but couldn't.

She'd left him at home just a couple hours earlier. Safe and sound. This couldn't be happening. She started panting as much from her recent exertions as in real panic. "Tell me you're nowhere near this." She struggled to draw in her next breath.

"I wish I could," the deep rumble of his breathy words came out sounding even more labored than hers, and she struggled to hear him over the sound of chaos in the background.

"After you left this morning, I got the call from the hospital…to help the first of the injured. Just got crazy after that. Listen to me. I love you…more than you will ever know…"

"No, no, no, no!" She lost it then. Started bawling as her vision blurred with sudden tears.

"Ssh…it's okay. It's gonna be okay. Please…just promise me…you'll remember our love, keep the faith…no matter what. It's a Godsend. I will love you forev–"

The line went dead.

"No-ooo! Joey! Joey!" She screamed his name at her wrist. "Jo–"

WHAM!

The next explosion hit her full force. Threw her up into the air and back several feet. Arms spread out at her sides; it felt like she was flying. And rather than the bone crushing force of the blast, and return to the hard pavement, instead, she felt a rare warmth enfold her. Like encircling arms, something leaned her backward as she glided in mid-air, and in slow motion… Then turned her? Just as a patch of grass near one of the many decorative fountains came into view. Tucked into fetal position, she tumbled and rolled over and over as she landed on the padded earth. Anxious hands gripped her as she fought to sit up. Propping herself up with one hand, she pressed the other to her head as she felt a shooting pain in her temple.

"Miss? You okay?" She heard a man's voice, just barely, over the loud whistling sound and a ringing in her ears that wouldn't go away. She grasped his proffered arm and tried to stand.

All the while thinking – How in the hell had she survived that? She majored in bomb construction and disarmament at the Academy. It was her specialty, so she knew what an explosion of that magnitude did to a body at close range.

She should be dismembered.

And dead.

"Oh my God, you're bleeding! Someone please… Get help! Call Sky-Med!"

She heard her helper's voice as though from a great distance.

"Oh…" She moved the hand that was on her head to her aching side and felt only mild surprise when she looked down and saw it covered in blood.

"Call my husband…a doctor…he'll know what to do," she whispered…then collapsed.

Affected to a degree he hadn't expected, given what he knew of her bright and blessed future, Jarit fought to contain his own deep sorrow in the moment. Stood close by and watched as the medical practitioners began their work on her.

He watched and waited.

Lent her whatever support he could. Then and later, through her deep crisis of faith.

He prayed…and stayed, with her…

Chapter 2

2 Samuel 14:20
...and my lord is wise, according to the wisdom of an angel of God, to know all things that are in the earth...

It wasn't true...what people said.

Time didn't really heal all wounds.

Instead, in Dani's thirty-eight years of experience, it still hurt every bit as much each time she allowed herself to dwell on Joe's absence, and the circumstances that led to it. The agony of it all was suffocating, robbing her of breath, and diminishing her will to live.

Oh, the agony–

Of recalling verbatim, what turned out to be his very last words. Of waking up in the hospital to hear that he was really gone. Of his memorial. Of having nothing of his, or hers, when she relocated to New York because their apartment was obliterated in one of the blasts. All of it. Each came flooding back in an excruciating, heart wrenching, roiling sea of emotional anguish.

It was just that some days, as time wore on, she didn't think about him every nano second, of the entire day.

Plus, over the last five years, since he passed, she'd learned to filter.

She could successfully push the soul crushing memories way down deep, and allow only the lighter, more manageable ones to surface, from time to time.

Because no matter how painful the memory, she'd never allow herself to forget him. Would never take friends' advice to subject herself to that new-fangled 'memory conditioning' that was becoming so popular with those who sought out a surgical solution for dealing with their grief.

No, she'd never forget him. Plus, he'd probably haunt her if she tried. She let out a little giggle as she got ready for bed.

She still remembered the very first day she laid eyes on him at her elementary school…

He'd just transferred in from another state. A scrawny little kid sitting all alone, having lunch in the cafeteria at the table across from hers.

"Hey kid…"

He looked up at her and then behind him, over his shoulder. He turned back, eyebrows raised over wide, unusual, crystal gray-blue eyes, he pointed to his chest.

"Yeah, you." She nodded. "You gonna eat that, or what?" She gestured to the untouched cupcake on the food tray in front of him.

"It's got nuts in it." His voice was soft, and he sounded nervous.

"So…?"

"So, I'm allergic."

She got up from her table and went over to his.

Sat on the end of the bench he was on, and then slid along until she was seated right next to him.

"Allergic?" She'd heard grown-ups say that some people didn't eat certain foods because of their religion. "So, is that like Jewish, or Jehovah's Witness, or something?"

"Naw." He gave a little shake of his head. "It's when you get sick from eating something that your body can't handle."

"Oh? Well, guess I'm allergic too then, 'cause I throw up every single time I eat too many donuts." She grinned, then giggled.

"No, that's just from over-eating." He shook his head, then laughed with her, not looking so nervous anymore. "This is much more serious than that. It's about being really super sensitive to things in the environment that are completely harmless to everyone else. Some people get red, itchy skin, or they get breathless. In extreme cases, even to the point where their throat closes up, and they stop breathing."

She wasn't sure she'd understood the half of what he said, but his voice was so impassioned, his youthful gaze so intense, she found herself completely drawn into his orbit.

"Wow…"

He nodded vigorously.

"I'm telling you, if I eat this–" he pointed to the cupcake, "–I could like literally die. See?" He tapped his watch a couple times and picked one of the files that popped out of it. He dragged it to rest on the table between them, turned to a marked screen and then slid it towards her.

"Wow..." She flipped a few more screens and saw the near encyclopedia of information he was so casually carrying around, on not just the subject of allergies, but what looked to her to be a whole bunch of other medical conditions as well.

She pushed it back to him. "You know way too much about all this stuff, kid. Trust me. You're never gonna make friends around here if you keep that up."

"That's okay, I'm used to it." He squared his shoulders and shrugged, but she thought he looked just the tiniest bit sad.

"When I grow up, they're all gonna come begging to be friends with me... Joseph Almonzo." He looked down at the table. Said it in such a low, yet determined voice, she almost didn't hear him.

"Oh yeah? And how do you figure that, *Joseph Almonzo*?"

"Isn't it obvious?" He looked up again and directly into her eyes. "It's clear to me, just like a shooting star, across the dark night sky... I'm gonna be a world-famous doctor." He said it with such pride and resolve, she felt just the tiniest bit envious.

"Well, good luck with that." She rose from her seat as the school alert system sounded, whistling shrilly throughout the large room. Along with the AI declaring–

"End of lunch break, children. Please return to your designated classroom immediately."

"You're a weird one Joe, that's for sure." She shook her head at him.

"Maybe," he shrugged. "But wanna eat lunch right here with me tomorrow?" His voice was bright. He stood, picked up the chocolate and almond covered cupcake, and held it out to her with a crooked little smile wreathing his adorable face.

She hesitated, then took it.

"We'll see." She took a big bite and grinned.

And from that day, until his last, they'd been practically inseparable.

She shook her head on a smile, as she fluffed her pillows and climbed into bed. Yep, he def was the most unusual kid she'd ever met. But he turned out to be her best friend in the whole world, and eventually, the greatest love of her life. She settled in, turned onto her back, pulled up the covers, and laced her fingers behind her head.

There was just something about him, even then. A maturity well beyond his years, and as they grew older, an intense charisma and magnetism that just lured her in, the more she was around him. They'd only been apart long-term for the time that he was away in medical school and she, at the police academy and on-the-job training. But even then, they'd kept in constant touch, so much so that the next time they saw each other in person was on their wedding day, and then when they really reconnected during their honeymoon…

And what a honeymoon it was.

Her body felt warm…tingled all over, at the vivid, intoxicating memory.

If only they hadn't decided to settle in New Atlantis, things would surely have turned out different. But the compensation in almost every industry in the alien-made city was phenomenal. Garnering them both double what they could have earned otherwise. And with his plan to start his own practice…well…it just seemed logical.

Until fate intervened.

She never got to share her amazing news. Had kept putting it off due to their busy schedules. Then, when she was finally going to tell him during a romantic rendezvous, she'd planned for that very night…

She hadn't just lost the love of her life on that terrible, fateful day. She'd lost their unborn daughter too.

Her career as a police officer was just starting to take off when she found out she was going to be a mother. Just when she was so sure she was going to make Detective too, so for just the briefest of moments, to her eternal shame, she'd thought the situation inconvenient, and even contemplated not keeping the child.

So, maybe God was punishing her?

No. She dismissed that thought almost immediately. From what she remembered of Sunday school when she was a child, and later from going to services with Joe, she knew that God loved her and would always be merciful.

She just wasn't sure if she could ever forgive herself.

It was all so tragic. Joe would have made such an awesome dad for Zoey too – her last coherent thought, as she drifted off to a fitful sleep.

"I've told her to expect you, Michael. Well–you as Svikari. And I also planted a mustard seed of faith, just as the Redeemer advised."

"Yes," the Archangel nodded. His expression grim. "It has already begun to bear fruit. Legion will target her now–try to unearth and destroy it. Root and stem. To say nothing of the looming threat she presents to them. They don't yet know, but from what's been revealed to me, she's about to become the catalyst for a faith-filled resistance like they've never seen before. Who's her guardian?"

"Jarit."

He nodded.

"He can stand down while I'm with her, but when I'm not, he knows to be alert to a new level of danger to her, yes?"

"Already done."

"Thank you, Alcindor."

"Which tactic will they employ initially?"

"Alien abduction. Men prefer to believe the author of lies - that some off-planet entity is pulling them from their beds. At best, they convince themselves and others that their minds are playing tricks on them. Anything but the truth–that they are engaged in an ongoing war for their very souls. A war that can only be won when they allow God in, to transform their hearts and lives with His light–a light every bit as real as the evil invading their dreams."

"I'll make sure Jarit knows. He's also already aware that a reveal like I did with Rissa is off the table for now."

Michael nodded.

"The Redeemer knows best given where she's at

in her journey…she's not ready for that yet. But everything has been set in motion, so we must be vigilant."

"Understood." Alcindor nodded.

"Whatever happens…one thing is certain. There is no going back for her now…"

Chapter 3

Ezekiel 36:25
Then will I sprinkle clean water upon you, and ye shall
be clean: from all your filthiness, and from all your
idols, will I cleanse you…

How freaky was this?

Dani was standing in the center of a dimly lit living room, looking around at furnishings she didn't recognize.

"So, ready for that drink now?"

She spun about.

"Say what?"

A man was approaching from a nearby doorway.

Wait…was that…Charlie Swift?

"I've got ice cold beer in the fridge, or I can get you something *harder*…if you prefer."

Wait…did he just…?

What…in the actual–factual f–

"Just say the word–" he interrupted her internal dialogue and stared at her, "–and your wish…is my command." He strolled forward; a smarmy smile plastered on his face.

A recruit she'd had the misfortune of encountering during her first year at the police academy, Charlie Swift had given her no end of grief as he pursued her relentlessly, refusing to take no for an answer, despite her many polite protests. Fortunately for her, as she recalled, he couldn't hack it and had been axed in under six months, before they'd even completed basic Verndari training.

"Uh…Charlie? What is this? Where are we?" She looked around as she backed up a bit, trying to remember how she'd got there.

"In my home, of course. I can't believe you finally took me up on my offer to have a drink." He was closing in on her. Getting far too close for her comfort.

"I what?! Look–" she held up her hands to halt his approach, "–not sure how I got here, but I've been nothing but civil with you. It's like I've said a hundred times. No, means no, okay? So, before I have to kick your sorry butt all up and down your nice little place here–" she gestured to indicate the space they were in, "you better back the hell off, so I can get on up outta here."

He stopped a few feet away, his face becoming a sudden mask of scary rage.

"Well…then I'm real sorry you feel that way, *Detective*."

What…?

He reached down to his waist, pulled out a gun she'd obviously failed to notice, and before she could react, aimed it right at her head and fired, at point blank range.

With stunning clarity, she heard the gun shot, saw the weapon recoil within his grasp. By pure reflex she raised her hands, palms facing outward in a futile attempt to ward off the danger. But rather than the life ending impact to her skull that she knew to expect, instead, she heard a droning buzz, felt the fluttering impact against her hands of…

Flies?

Dozens of them. Then hundreds. In a constant flowing stream. Out they came, from the barrel of the weapon he still had trained on her head.

"What the hell?"

Beginning to wave her arms around, she swatted at the offending insects as they surrounded her. Turning, she spotted the front door and made a run for it. Grasping the antique handle, she yanked it open. Squinting, she raised a hand to shield her eyes from the sudden glare of the unexpected bright sunlight beyond the door. Hearing his maniacal laughter follow her out, but thankfully not the insect plague, she bounded down a handful of steps, sprinted along a short walkway, then pushed open a small gate, that let her out onto an empty street.

Taking a moment to catch her breath, she propped her hands on her thighs, looked down and then looked up, gasping as a sight a short distance to the left drew her disbelieving gaze in that direction, and upwards.

Up, and then up some more, she stared. Not at buildings, but at the enormous rocky edges of half a dozen humongous statues of ancient deities of worldly religions. Spaced a short distance apart they stood, like mountain ranges in a straight line. Each one menacing everything on the ground beneath them, by their sheer magnitude. Their pinkish sandstone formations towered above her, ominous in the way they reached up into the bright blue sky.

All of a sudden, at the very tops of each, a rumbling started. Low at first and then climbing in volume and intensity, as their heads and faces began to crack, and then to crumble. Tons of stone and dust rolled, and then came crashing down their rocky sides.

Fascinated by the sight, but yet still terrified, a new realization broke through her worried mind, that she could soon be buried under the avalanche. Heart pounding in her chest, she turned to her right and bolted. Fleeing along the street, and glancing back over her shoulder as she ran, she headed in the opposite direction of the horrendous destruction, as fast as her feet would carry her. Coming to a dead end, she turned right again into a quiet street and found herself in an oasis by comparison. For where before there had been nothing but dry, dusty ground, here now was lush tropical beauty.

Here and there, fountains of water gurgled with sweet musical tones. Their life-giving liquid irrigating the thick, dark green, leafy foliage that graced the front of elegant, classically styled buildings that were positioned on either side of a quaint cobbled walkway.

As she caught her breath, she looked to her left and noticed at least a half dozen statues, set into the shrubbery at intervals all along the path. This time they were of man-sized, multi winged angels, made from the finest chiseled granite.

She walked over and stood, to take a closer look at the first. A sudden, brisk breeze blew a spray of the nearby fountain's cool water on her, refreshing her for but a moment as she admired the craftmanship in his outstretched wings. So intricate and life-like she half expected him to take flight, right before her eyes. With head bowed, his hands were clasped before him in reverent pose.

"Pray..."

She spun in a full circle, as she felt as much as heard the single word, in a whisper, all around her.

Curious, when nothing else happened with the first, on pure instinct she stepped to the right, to the second angel in the line. Wings also outstretched, he too was looking down, but this time, at a book.

"Read...the Word..." Once again, the whispered recommendation flowed through and around her, invoking a pleasant feeling of peace and contentment. Inhaling deep, she could swear the air around her was suddenly perfumed with the most amazing and intoxicating fragrance she'd ever smelt in her life.

Eager to see what wisdom the next angel would impart; she stepped across to the third.

Huh...?

Unlike the others, his arms and wings were down and close at his sides, and while his head was upright, his eyes were closed, as though he was asleep.

Wonder what that means...

She stood for a moment, in utter silence. Then she heard it, another whisper, but this time indistinct, far softer than the others, and with no accompanying pleasant sensations. She couldn't be sure, but it sounded to her like...

Not yet...

Disappointed, she stepped in closer until she was almost nose to neck with him, thinking that surely her close proximity would encourage a response more like the first two.

"Hullo?"

His eyelids raised then, ever so slowly. Second by agonizing second, until…

She was captured…in the penetrating gaze of her husband's eyes. Real. Striking. Unmistakable. Crystal clear, gray-blue. Looking out at her…from the face of an angel.

"Oh my God… Joey?" she gasped–

And heard the end of her sharp intake of breath, as she sat bolt upright in bed.

Just waaaayy too much 21st century TV…right?
"Yeah, that must be it."

Wondering about the cause of her bizarre night, Dani dragged herself into the precinct squad room that morning like a drunk with a bad hangover.

But it had all seemed so real…

Barely acknowledging the greetings of her colleagues as she made her way over to the floating beverage station for a bracing cup, she shook her head to free it of the lingering images of massive god-sized rock formations, granite angel wings, and buzzing–

Flies?

I mean, seriously? Like, what the actual–

fluttering f–

"Stop cussing, stop cussing…" She tapped her forehead with a finger and chanted her mantra under her breath, to stop the next foul word from popping into her thoughts–

"You're so much better than that, Dani."

Even as Joe's determined words and the image of his encouraging smile, and now haunting gray eyes, played in her mind.

She grabbed her coffee, dropped into the chair at her desk, and got set to be buried in a mountain of paperwork for the next several hours, if not days. Given the three pending reports she had to complete, plus her heavy case load, she wasn't so sure she'd ever get to see daylight again.

Like that crazy rogue defender case. What in the H-E-and-two-sticks was she supposed to write to adequately explain that. Maybe she could just–

"Good morning, Detective Almonzo."

Startled, she looked up, just as she was taking the first sip from her mug.

"Verndari, call me…Svikari. I understand you've been looking for me."

Chapter 4

Deuteronomy 20:4
For the Lord your God is He that goeth with you, to fight
for you against your enemies, to save you...

Dani choked on her hot sip of coffee, plunked down the mug, grabbed up a glass from her side table and took a hasty sip of water to cool her throat…

Along with the rest of her.

Ooo-we…! Well, damn Mr. Svikari…aren't you just a tall drink of hot and tasty Caucasian…

Verndari sure made 'em big.

A memory of the other one she'd seen at fairly close range in New Atlantis flashed into her mind. About six foot seven, this one was fashionably dressed, blond, gorgeous, and built like an Abrams battle tank.

And that voice…

All velvety, with just a hint of an accent. It was a tried and true, drop-your-panties kind of deep rumble.

Aw yeah…a tall ride for sure…just make yuh wanna jump on and–

His left brow rose, and his lips curved–both, for like a nano second. Not quite a smile, but maybe more of an attractive twitch? If she hadn't done that training in how to recognize and read micro-expressions she might have missed it. And, if she didn't know any better, she'd have said it was in response to what she'd been thinking.

Reflexively, she pulled herself up in her chair, straightened her jacket, and pushed her coffee mug to the side, even as she chastised herself for being such a complete idiot. True, she didn't know very much about the alien co-inhabitants of their planet, but she was pretty sure they weren't mind readers.

"Ah…good morning to you too, and thanks so much for coming in, in response to our request last week."

He nodded, just once.

"However, as it turns out, we actually closed the case we thought you could assist us with, so I'm afraid I need to apologize on behalf of the department for wasting your time."

"Not necessary at all. Especially since I've also come on another matter. I believe you've met my friend Al?"

"Sorry…who?"

He placed his palms flat on her desk and leaned in closer. "Al."

After taking a moment to admire his long fingers with their well-manicured nails, she lifted her gaze and was snared in his bright blue one.

Light dawned.

"Oh…of course, Al…right. Please," she indicated the chair next to her desk, "take a seat."

"Thank you." He pulled it back slightly, swung a long, powerful looking leg around and sat.

Damn! Even the way he moved was a huge turn on – just a master class of manly grace meets precision and economy of movement. She picked up her glass and took another long cool sip.

So…*this* was the defender Al had told her to expect?

How in the hell had a little, old, black guy like that *ever* have occasion to get to know the blond bombshell sitting at her desk right now.

"So…you and Al, huh? Just curious…how exactly did you two get acquainted?"

"I'm in PR, so my job allows me to meet many…at different times along their journey."

"Uh-huh…" She tapped a fingernail on the desk in front of her a few times.

He was being honest, she felt sure, but yet still, something told her, not telling her the half of it.

Yep. Just call him vague-a-licious, because he'd def just whet her appetite for more.

"And…tell me…is there a Mrs. Svikari?" She popped up her brows for a second and let her tongue just graze her top lip as she offered him her most sultry smile.

This time his left brow climbed almost to his hairline…and stayed there. He looked…confused and even a bit uncomfortable? If she had to guess.

"Tell *me,* Detective, are you always this…direct?" He gave her a slight smile.

"What can I say? Occupational hazard." She tilted her head to the side and lifted both palms, indicating their surroundings. "Shyness and subtlety don't exactly cut it around here."

"Indeed," he nodded.

He hadn't answered her question. Had instead asked her one of his own. She knew what that meant. Had read the signs, loud and clear.

So, she'd swung and missed. So what? It was still worth the try. Just look at him for God's sake. She felt obligated to at least make a play for him.

Maybe he didn't go for strong women. She could respect that. And, truthfully, she didn't even know what she'd have done next if he *had* picked up what she was putting down. She nearly snorted. Hell, she hadn't even been out on a date, far less a date-date, since Joe died. She recalled the cute phrase they'd come up with as teenagers to signify a serious relationship.

Mentally she shook herself. Back to business then.

"Right. So, Al mentioned you might have something to share that I might find interesting."

"Yes."

When he didn't say more, she raised her brows to urge him to continue.

"Perhaps we should discuss this in a more…private setting?" He looked to the left, then to the right of the squad room. "Where you'd be less…distracted."

"No need. It's…uh–" she glanced at Detective Robert Dorran who'd moved from his desk to stand directly behind Svikari, and then wished she hadn't as he grinned and wiggled his eyebrows suggestively. He straightened up in record time, even turned to look in the opposite direction as Svikari glanced back over his shoulder.

"–uh, on second thought, yeah, let's take this to

a conference room.

"What are you, Dorran? Like ten?" She whispered only for his ears and punched him in the arm as she paused beside him, on her way to check the e-register on the wall for a free space.

"Ow." He rubbed the spot. "Good arm, Monzo. Don't hurt him now." He grinned, his voice low and provocative. He barked out a laugh and turned back to his desk, after she fake-grinned and showed him 'the finger'.

She ran the same hand over her hair when she caught sight of Svikari's now familiar raised eyebrow and lip quirk, then pointed to guide him in the direction of the empty room she'd just booked for the next hour.

"Sorry about that little lapse in there. The guys here can get a bit–ah–scandalous, sometimes. Just blowing off steam." She ushered him to a seat at the table in the space and turned on the maximum privacy setting for good measure before sitting opposite him.

"No need to explain. I can imagine how stressful this environment can be for you."

"You have no idea." She shook her head. "So, where were we?"

"Yes. Cards on the table. I'm privy to certain sensitive information, of which I believe the human population should be made aware. Obviously, as an outsider, there are places where I just can't go, while you on the other hand, would easily gain entry. Whether in your professional, or even personal capacity. I'm prepared to share intel with you, on a need-to-know basis, so you can help me to safeguard certain persons in key positions of the US government that I know to be targets of Verndari."

"Uh-huh." She rocked back in her chair, digested his words and decided on her first question. "Safeguard them from what exactly? Assassination?"

"Worse."

"What's worse than murder?"

"Hosting."

"Say what?" Her mind reeling, she jerked forward, hoping she'd misunderstood.

"You heard me right. It's where Verndari take over a human host to control them." His expression was one of righteous rage. "They're still in there, but they're in torment, unable to communicate, or regain control of their own bodies."

"Okay, well that's different. Wasn't expecting that," she tried to sound casual, while for the second time in twenty-four hours, in her mind she was standing, waving her arms around and screaming–

What in the actual bleeeep!

"I know it's a lot to take in–"

"Oh really? Yuh think so, Svik?!" She tilted her head to the side, her stare locking in on his bright blue one.

He graced her with a very attractive half of a smile this time.

On anyone else it would have been underwhelming, but somehow, coming from him, it was stunning. Current dilemma aside, his unexpected expression of joy made the revelation seem far less cataclysmic.

Sure, she was just as eager as the next do-gooder

to protect the future of mankind and all, but come on! Alien possession? And who knew what other crap. She def hadn't signed up for any of that.

"Like I said, yes. It's a lot, but if you allow them to get a foothold now, it's going to be that much harder to beat them back later, when things get really sticky. Think about it, if they get control of certain key senators–"

"They could control the Senate, the Congress and eventually even the Presidency, the last bastion of global democracy. Yeah, yeah. No need to paint a picture. Devastation of epic proportions. I got that part. So, what about you and others like you? I assume there are others?"

He nodded, but didn't elaborate.

"If and when your scary, body-inhabiting friends get wind of what you've been doing–working against them? What happens to you?"

"Give no thought to me, Detective. I can handle myself."

"No doubt."

And she absolutely believed him.

It wasn't so much in his words, as it was about the way he said them–no pride or pretense of any kind. Just a statement of simple, undeniable fact.

"And here's the last part," she leaned forward, "the part where you tell me - What's in it for you?"

"In a word–satisfaction."

She flicked her hands open atop the table, gave him a look she hoped would prompt him to elaborate.

"The satisfaction of setting a wrong, right, Detective.

"My…colleagues. They were once like me.

They had the best interests of mankind at heart a long time ago. But that changed. They became self-serving, vindictive, vengeful, and vicious false gods. I'm here to help you balance the scales.

"I promise, you can trust me." He leaned forward, mirroring her pose. "So, I'm asking…will you help me, to help mankind before it's too late?"

She saw the intensity in his focused blue gaze. Heard the sincerity in his impassioned plea. There was no question in her mind he was telling her the truth, but…the specter of her experience in New Atlantis, the death of her husband, and the role that his kind may, or may not, have played in that tragedy, all rose up in her mind and stopped her short, leaving her cold.

She looked down at her hands resting on the table. At the only piece of jewelry, she ever wore. The wedding ring Joe had so carefully placed on her finger, entrusted to her along with his heart. A treasured symbol of their love.

And just like that, she was transported–to the place of despair she fought so hard to avoid.

"I think I understand why you may be hesitant to trust in something so…unfamiliar. To revive your faith in anything…when you feel so betrayed. Like all you hold dear is lost." his voice was soft.

Her gaze snapped up. His climbed to hers more slowly, a few long seconds after it shifted away from her left hand.

He looked at her. His face, the very picture of compelling compassion.

How could he know?

Stunned, she lowered her left hand to rest on her

thigh, beneath the table, but still met his stare.

"Talk to me, Detective." His eyes searched hers, darting back and forth. "I sense you need to unburden. Why not free yourself, here and now, from these shackles that bind you. This is a safe space. Whatever you say will never leave this room, and I promise, you will be the better for it."

She blinked back the tears that threatened to betray her practiced stoicism.

Hesitated…until…

"It was five years ago," she let out a shaky breath. Cleared her throat. Searched her mind for a short version of her painful story she could share, against her better judgement. And not at all sure if her intention was about protecting her privacy from a virtual stranger, or more about sparing herself the raw anguish of the full tale.

"I was stationed with the New Atlantis PD. Lost my husband in the chaos when the domes cracked. Was told he was probably at ground zero of one of the bigger blasts." She blew out a whistling breath, shook her head and tried to steady her voice, as she heard it crack. "'Cause they…ah…" another breath, "…they never actually recovered his body. You can't exactly search the Atlantic, can you?" She tried to not sound bitter, swiped at her cheek, to rid it of an escaped tear. Compressed her lips to make them quit trembling.

She sat up straighter against the back of her chair. Put her head back and looked up at the light fixture set into the ceiling high above the table. Feeling more in control she looked back towards him.

"I saw this guy at one of the buildings that was destroyed that morning. He said he was a defender. It looked like he pushed something into the wall?" She shrugged. "I couldn't get a good look at it but–"

"High precision, penetrating explosive."

"You've seen one?"

"Many.

"It's one of the secret weapons Verndari has been employing, here in the US and around the world, to cause chaos and destabilize sitting governments. There was a human scientist, on par with other notables like Newton and Einstein. He was working with them initially until he uncovered some of the more, shall we say, unsavory aspects of their activities. He would have revealed to the world that they've been secretly creating weapons like that one…of unimaginable destruction; that would make the devastation of Hiroshima look like a scratch bomb in comparison. He and a handful of his associates created special technology that would have proved dangerous to them, uncovering their ability to inhabit a human… among other things. They managed to escape to New Atlantis but were lured out from where they were in hiding, scattered around the city.

"Verndari built that city and fortified it with an intricate network of energy shields, stacked side by side, and one on top of the other. Trip one circuit and certain sections of the domes will just collapse in on each other, like a house of cards. They planted those explosives, very strategically. They knew precisely what they needed to do to eliminate those scientists and the tech they created, simply to cover their tracks.

"Five dead scientists just out of the blue would raise unwarranted attention but an unfortunate accident involving a conflagration of explosions, and sections of shield and dome failures, like dominoes falling. That proved to be just the ideal kind of chaos that would allow them to continue on with their covert agenda."

"All that devastation, so many thousands killed, collateral damage so they could get to just a few people?" Horror and disbelief struggled for precedence in her mind.

"And…they don't just use the weapons themselves, they also sell to terrorist groups, competing factions, and under the table to clandestine government agencies around the world. They're not discerning, other than having the aim of causing maximum chaos. They hold auctions on the dark web and then sell to the highest bidder."

"Well, of course, they do." She barked out a harsh laugh. "And to think, my A-hole bosses in the NAPD made me feel like I was crazy. Like I didn't see what I *knew* I saw." She compressed her lips again. This time, to control the anger welling up inside of her as her mind raced with conspiracy theories, that one or more of them may have been in on the entire plot, with the rogue defenders.

"If we're really going to do this. I'd have to read in my immediate boss - Detective Superintendent Duncan Wright."

"You trust him?"

"With my life."

He nodded.

"Well, it's decided then." She nodded in turn. "I guess there's nothing left to say except, take my hand and welcome me to the revolution, comrade." She stood and extended it to him across the table.

He shook it. His expression, grim.

Chapter 5

Proverbs 18:15
The heart of the prudent getteth knowledge; and the ear
of the wise seeketh knowledge…

"So, let me get this straight. This Svikari guy, he came here? Looking for you?"

Dani nodded.

"And you should have seen him. He just walked right in, like freakin' G.I. Joe in a business suit. All buff and tasty. Ooo-Weee!! Just built. Like a damn GQ-holo, I mean just–"

"All right, all right…I got it Monzo," detective superintendent Duncan Wright held up a hand. "No need to paint me a picture."

She stopped short of fanning herself, just barely, as the vivid memory of six feet seven inches of alien perfection returned.

Detective Wright shook his dark blond head, as a muscle in his jaw tightened.

She couldn't be sure, and she didn't know why, but she thought he looked pissed.

"So anyway, we have a mutual acquaintance who figured we could help each other. I'm telling you Wright, we're onto something really big here."

She stretched her arms wide. "I mean, like we barely scratched the surface in our investigation when it comes to the Verndari threat level. We're getting real close to something that's gonna blow this whole thing wide open. I can feel it." She filled him in on the conversation she had with Svikari in that very room in which they now sat.

He rose from his seat, began pacing the length of the space in front of the table, back and forth, like a caged animal.

"So, you're telling me they can inhabit a human's body? Just take over, virtually anybody at any time?"

She nodded.

"I gotta say…this is starting to sound like it's way above my pay grade, Monzo." He stopped right opposite her. Ran a hand through the thick waves of his dark blond hair, then placed his palms flat down on the table. He pinned her with his blue gaze. "Maybe we need to kick this up the chain."

"Are you crazy? And tell them what, Detective?" She opened her palms and searched his eyes for a moment. "That on the say-so of some rando, rogue defender we may or may not have uncovered the greatest threat to humanity the world has ever seen?

"Look, just hear me out. How about we see what evidence he brings us first, do a little digging of our own. You know, just to make sure it's legit, and then see where this goes."

"Follow Alice down the rabbit hole?"

"Sure." She shrugged. "Or at least part of the way down."

"You'd better be right about this, Monzo, or–"
"It's both our asses... Trust and believe, I know."
She blew out a noisy breath.
"Yeah, exactly," he echoed the breath.

Chapter 6

Song of Solomon 7:10
I am my beloved's, and his desire is toward me…

"**Well, damn, Joey**. Just look at you… When did you get all buff and tasty? Just starrin'…like a GQ-holo. HA!" Dani barked out a laugh.

She crossed her arms over her chest and made a show of licking her lips, as she let her gaze take the scenic route–from the thick black waves of his hair, over his handsome face and past his perfect pecs and biceps, shown off to chiseled perfection by the gray sweater she'd got him to match his eyes. And lower, to a muscled abdomen, long powerful looking legs encased in casual black jeans, right on down to his stylish booted feet.

The scrawny kid she'd befriended all those years earlier was certainly gone. No doubt. Because in his place, stood six feet three of primo, A-grade, thirst-trap.

He smiled slow and shook his head as he glanced down at his feet.

"Is that your way of saying you missed me?" His familiar deep masculine rumble washed over and through her, even as his smoky gray gaze returned to hers. "I've missed you too, Dani. Come 'ere." He grinned, as he pulled her into a bear hug. She shrieked and then laughed with him as he lifted her clear off the ground, swung her around and into his apartment.

He kicked the antique door shut and set her down as she took in a deep breath.

"Mm…is that your mom's lasagna and garlic bread I smell?"

"With a twist." He nodded.

"Of course. I wouldn't expect anything less from you." She walked backward for a few steps as she grinned at him, then turned and made a beeline straight for the kitchen.

Despite his age, due to his advanced intellect, Joe was already into his third year of medical school and was renting an apartment near campus. She'd been away for four months on a college trip to the moon's new lunar science station. An opportunity of a lifetime, she grasped with both hands, given her free time before she headed to the police academy in the spring of the following year.

"Thanks Joey. That was the best meal I've had in months." She patted her stomach after they finished dinner.

"Real high praise considering you've been on the moon, eating freeze-dried rations, so–"

"Like hell." She gave a vigorous shake of her head. "I'll have you know we had a couple of those fancy, new replicators that dispense synthesized food. So instead of fake, freeze-dried food, it tasted like fake, reconstructed food." She clapped her hands together and gave him a cheeky grin as she giggled.

"So, like I started to say, anything would taste great after that." His tone was dry, but she caught his quirky smile as he eyed her over the top of his glass.

"Aw, come on now…you know what I meant." She rolled her eyes. "You know how much I crave your good, down-home cooking and yes, I'll say it again. You missed your calling. For real." She looked at her plate and resisted the urge to lick off the remaining streaks of delicious, Italian-Thai flavored sauce. "You should be in culinary school, working on being a world-famous chef, not a doctor."

He shook his head. "No way. As you well know, medical research, healing the sick and the injured, that's my true God-given purpose in this world, this–" he lifted some of the leftovers, walked over to the fridge and deposited them inside, "–is just a hobby I enjoy, and that I happen to be good at."

"Yeah, yeah." She nodded as she too rose from the table, picked up the rest of the tossed salad and joined him in front of the fridge. He held the door open for her.

"I hear yuh. Just as long as I get to keep reaping the benefits of your little hobby–" she squeezed in between him and the door and placed the bowl inside, on the shelf below the other two dishes, "–I'm good to go."

"Yeah…you sure are."

Thrown by an unfamiliar note she detected in his tone she looked back, just in time to see his gaze make a slow return from her butt to her eyes.

Like the sizzle in the atmosphere during an

electrical storm. Just like that. She felt a palpable shift in the room.

Uncertain, she avoided touching him as she closed the fridge door, turned and moved away to lean against his kitchen counter, on the opposite side of where he stood.

He gave her a look. His eyes turning smoky gray-blue. He took two long, slow steps towards her, then another. Ran his hands from her shoulders, down her arms, once he got there. Held onto her fingers and peered down at her, as she looked up.

His head inched lower…

"Now, I know you're not planning on kissing me right now, are you, Doc?" She tried a small laugh, but inside she felt unprepared. And shaky. Nervous, she detached their hands, sidestepped around him, and walked back to the fridge. This time she stood about a foot from the wall to the left of it. Half afraid he'd follow her. Instead, he turned, leaned back against the section of the counter she'd just vacated, and crossed a casual booted foot over his ankle.

"Exactly how long are you planning to keep this up?" He shook his head. "Why don't you just give up the ghost, Dani."

"Say what?"

"Give it up. Whatever it is you're holding onto to justify keeping this careful distance between us." His words were calm, measured.

"What?" She snorted on a laugh. "All that working out must be affecting your brain, bro. We've been best friends, for like, forever. There's no distance between us."

"Okay, so it's not about trust, or love, because

you know. And I know. We've got that in spades.

"And it's not about your parents' divorce 'cause you're nothing like your mom. You know that. You couldn't be more different. You'd never leave like she did.

"And I def know it's not the age thing because you look so amazing." His gaze blazed a heated path from her head to her toes, and back up again. "People are always too taken with that…hmm…gorgeous–" he half growled–bit his lower lip, "–just bangin' bod of yours…*and* that pretty face, to even guess I'm a few years younger. Plus, you've never cared about that anyway.

"So, by my calc, that leaves exactly nothing. Absolutely zero reasons, for you to be keeping me at arm's length."

He uncrossed his feet. Pushed away from the counter and began a slow approach.

She felt her heart skip a beat, took a step back. Felt her butt hit the wall.

Damn, his small apartment…

"In fact, it's clear to me…like a shooting star…across the dark night sky…that somewhere inside that stubborn head of yours you've actually already accepted the truth. It's just that you won't get out of your own way, long enough to admit it."

He stood so close now, mere inches away.

She looked up…into his eyes.

Lost her breath.

"We're not kids anymore, Danielle." His deep, no-nonsense tone vibrated through her. "And playtime… is over.

"So why don't you just admit the truth–that I'm

exactly what you want. The *only* man, you'll ever want."

He reached out and placed both hands flat on the wall above her shoulders. Dropped his head, pinned her with his bright gaze.

"What? Did you think I wouldn't know?"

His eyes searched hers. And at first, she thought his had never been more captivating… At least until his gaze dropped…and then settled…on her mouth.

His tongue darted out, touched his top lip, and in her mind, he could already taste her…and she, him.

"I know everything about you, Dani, and I've had you…from the second I gave you that cupcake in elementary school."

Her gaze snapped up from his mouth and got snared in smoky gray-blue intent.

"You're mine, Dani. You've always. Been. Mine."

"Enough…" she breathed her acceptance. Reached up and grasped his head with both hands. Buried her fingers in the thick waves of his hair. Eager to taste him, she tiptoed up. Met him halfway, as their lips joined. Played. And then clung.

"Playtime's over…" She nodded, as they separated.

For but a moment, before she pulled his smiling lips down to hers, again.

Chapter 7

Psalms 55:5-6
Fearfulness and trembling are come upon me, and
horror hath overwhelmed me.
And I said, oh that I had wings like a dove! For then
would I fly away, and be at rest...

Dani struggled to lift her eyelids. Feeling diminished, like she'd been drugged, she searched her foggy mind, tried to latch onto her last memory–

Joe.

Their first real kiss…in his apartment.

Beyond that…she tried to recall, and failed.

In a prone position, she shifted. Alarmed when she found she couldn't move her head in any direction, more than to nod. Her arms and legs felt numb, heavy.

Her lids finally obeyed her command to open, but the result wasn't much of an improvement. Everything was a blur. Surrounded by near darkness mid-range, and a complete abyss further afield, she narrowed her focus and squinted, trying to see whatever it was that held her in such effective restraint.

Mere inches from her face and in her peripheral

vision she saw thick coils of wire in arches around her head and lower, circling and even puncturing her torso for as far as she could see.

What in the hell? Her lips moved as she said the words, but didn't emit a sound. She tried again and recognized she only gave voice to them in her increasingly troubled mind.

Feeling the onset of real panic, she forced herself to take deep breaths, calm down and further assess the physical threat. She tried to move once more, but only managed to roll a bit to her left and then back again.

Odd, but there was no blood that she could see, and she felt only mild pressure, rather than the agonizing pain she imagined she should have been in, given the crisscrossing of metal making her body into some kind of hybrid, metal-human spring. Stuck in a cramped position on her side, she began to jerk and wrestle with the contraption in earnest. Bouncing up and down a bit, she still only succeeded in rolling from side to side, just around the time she began to notice something else.

Jeering and cheering.

Hollow sounding, it drifted over to her as though from a far distance.

And as she alternately bounced, rolled and spun, she caught sight of them – one by one like someone kept switching on a series of dim spotlights overhead–the distorted shapes of dozens of onlookers came into indistinct view.

Standing in groups of varying numbers all around her, as though she were their evening's entertainment. Some were pointing, laughing, even egging her on in her struggle to be free. While still another set, though clearly far fewer in number, looked at her with pity. At least when they weren't looking behind them, their faces becoming masks of anxiety and bleak ineptitude.

And then she heard it, an anxious female voice, but strangely not with her ears. Instead, it echoed, in her head, similar to her own thoughts.

"Will no one help her?"

A voice, she felt sure was coming from the woman who just pushed through to the very front of the pity posse. Fuzzy, like looking through an unfocused rifle sight she couldn't quite make out her features, but she could tell she was brunette, casually dressed, average height and build.

She stepped forward and with laudable disregard for the mounting hostility now directed her way, she dropped to her knees, and while humming a catchy little tune, began to tug at the spiral restraints.

And the most amazing thing happened, whether from guilt or shame or both, two or three of the pity particrs stepped forward. Hesitant, they looked over their shoulders as though in fear of discovery. Working together as one, it wasn't long before they broke her free.

Dani pushed her shaky limbs to comply and managed to raise herself to a seated position. Her brave rescuer helped steady her, then began to stand herself as her voice again sounded in her mind.

"Another one like me. Wonder who she is…"

"Another one like what?" Dani went for broke and tried to respond with her own thoughts.

Her rescuer's gaze jerked to hers as she dropped

to her knees once more and leaned towards her.

"Oh my God I just heard that. Can you hear me?"

"Yeah, in my head, not sure how. What is this?"

With a quick twist of her head, she looked back, over her shoulder.

"No time, he'll be coming." She stood, and to Dani's surprise, with an ease born of obvious practice, she very gracefully lifted right off the ground. Hung in the air about six feet up like a 21st century cinematic superhero.

"Wait? What? Who's coming?" Her mind in a fog, the investigator in her clamored for answers as she sensed, and then saw, a sudden deepening of the surrounding darkness.

"Just pray, if you can't wake up." Dani heard as Superwoman turned in midair and then shot upward at a phenomenal rate of speed. She disappeared into the night sky.

Can't wake up...? What?

As the threatening darkness got deeper and began to close in on her, she looked around and realized she was now completely alone. But before she could react, she felt a rare comforting warmth surround her for just a moment. Then, in the very next instant, like being on the end of an elastic band, she was pulled backward, with tremendous force.

Her eyes snapped open. Breathing in short sharp gasps she looked around the dimness of her bedroom lit by a watery moon. Her comfy armchair. The multi-exercise apparatus cube like Joe's that she'd bought after his death, and never used. One by one, she searched out and found familiar items to help anchor her abrupt return to her accustomed reality.

What just happened? Verndari? Or some new species of alien abduction? Or was she simply losing her mind? She didn't know which of the three held less appeal.

Logic and the scientific side of her argued that none of what she'd just experienced could be real. Trouble was, it felt just as tangible to her, enough to be concerned she couldn't tell the difference.

This was twice now she'd found herself in a frightening, otherworldly environment. And one she knew by instinct was potentially life-threatening should she run out of timely escapes like she'd had tonight. So, what was she to do? What were her options?

In the circumstances, she could think of only one.

Leaning over to her bedside table she touched the top drawer, and it slid open. Reaching in, she pulled out the reader Joe had given her on their very first wedding anniversary. Something she hadn't been able to bring herself to look at in five years. She smiled, as she flipped a few screens to get to the marked page that had been his very favorite. She hesitated, then tapped on her preferred Avatar. She pointed the unit at her armchair.

A 3-D hologram of legendary actor James Earl Jones appeared right in front of her chair. He sat down and turned some pages in the book he was holding.

He looked up and gave her a familiar smile.

"This is a very good choice, Danielle," his rich, iconic baritone filled the empty space in her room.

"Let's begin, shall we?"

He looked down, and with his very distinct diction, started to read to her–

"In the beginning was the Word…and the Word was with God…and the Word was God…"

Chapter 8

Matthew 7:15
Beware of false prophets, which come to you in sheep's
clothing, but inwardly they are ravening wolves…

"Good morning, Detective."

About to stretch out her hamstrings on a bench after her morning run, Dani spun around in surprise at the unmistakable deep tone of Svikari's voice. Dressed from head to toe in Armani Privé, he looked like he just stepped off the runway, and into their fall e-catalogue.

Damn…

Shaking her head to free it of her less than pure thoughts, she considered his sudden appearance. She wasn't easy to track. She regularly and intentionally changed her route from one to another of the city's many less popular running zones. And thanks to the difficult night she'd had, today she'd started out at the crack of dawn.

"How in the world did you find me? And at this hour?" She consulted her timepiece for confirmation of how early it was.

"To save time, why don't you just assume I know most everything."

Again, with the quiet, confident, yet at the same time unassuming, statement of fact.

How in the H-E-and-two-sticks does he do that?

"We can't meet at your precinct too frequently. It may raise unwanted questions we aren't prepared to respond to just yet. So, I'll find you whenever I need to."

"Whenever? You're not gonna pop up in my shower tomorrow, are yuh?" She snorted on a short laugh.

No reaction. He didn't even crack a smile.

She decided to test a theory.

"So Svik," she eyed him. "Did you hear the one about the first restaurant they opened on the moon?"

He gave her a curious look and shook his head in response.

"It had great food…but no atmosphere." She barked out a laugh, reached up and grasped his massive bicep, draped in pricy haute couture, to encourage him to laugh with her.

"Get it?! 'Cause, yuh know…atmosphere is like ambiance…so…uh…No?" She took in his still blank expression and let her laughter die off.

"Wow…tough crowd." She made a show of releasing her grip on his arm and smoothed out a small crease she'd probably put in the fabric of his jacket. "So, what's up?"

"I have something I think might interest you." He looked down at her and got right to business. He reached into the pocket of his jacket extracted and then handed her a data dot in its tiny case. "I'll be in touch when I have more. Stay safe and blessed, Detective." He held her gaze. Delivered that last remark with more attention to her than he showed throughout their entire exchange. And before she could query it further, he turned on his heel and walked away, his pace, brisk.

"Okay, well…good talk. See you when I see yuh." She waved and raised her voice as he crossed the street and disappeared around the corner.

Stay blessed?

Well, if that wasn't *très* freaky, she didn't know what was. But given the night she'd had, she'd take it.

"That guy is just way too intense though. I'm gonna make him laugh…if it's the last thing I do," she vowed to herself and went back to stretching.

After a refreshing shower in the precinct's ladies' locker room, Dani approached Detective Wright, hard at work at his desk in the squad room.

"Got a minute detective?" As discretely as she could, she showed him the data dot she'd received that morning. His eyes widened and he nodded.

He rose and followed her to the same conference room they'd been meeting in since beginning to discuss their plans to unearth 'The Verndari Agenda' as she called it.

"What's on it?" He pulled out a chair and sat as soon as he switched on the maximum privacy mode.

"No clue, thought we'd discover that together." She pressed the loading button on the table and set the dot on the scanner that rose up from the center of it. "What's your pleasure? 2-D screen, 3-D, or the full Monty–in-your-face, reach out and touch it like you're there, cinematic experience?"

"Could be a damn horror show, Monzo. What do you think?" The mildly exasperated look he gave her spoke volumes.

"Good point. 2D it is." She pressed a few more buttons to set the parameters and mode for it to play on an air screen in front of them.

As they watched, several people in evening wear began walking in and out of a well-appointed room.

"Where is that?"

"Think it's a receiving room in Verndari Diplomatic Center. I've been once or twice. I recognize the odd-looking wall decoration. See?" He pointed.

She leaned forward in her chair, touched the screen to pause the footage, then used her thumb and forefinger to expand the view of the wall he indicated. "What in the actual H-E-and-two-sticks…?"

"Really? H-E and what?" He barked out a laugh. "What are you, like ten?"

"Gimme a break, Detective. I'm trying to clean up my language."

He held up his hands in surrender and chuckled. "Well, good for you. Whatever works, I guess."

"Seriously though, is that…what I think it is?" She looked back at the screen and pointed.

"Yep," he nodded. "Pics of big, steaming piles and smears of–"

"Oh…crap…" She pulled her hand back to

cover her mouth.

"Exactly." He rocked back in his chair and squinted at the screen.

"Damnedest thing I've ever seen. Heard someone say it signifies fruitfulness to them. I guess because it fertilizes plants and crops and stuff?"

She turned her strongest look of incredulity on him.

"Trying to give them the benefit of the doubt here. It's an entirely different culture, remember." He shrugged.

"More likely it's their stock in trade." She shuddered as she got a frightening flash of dozens of them wallowing and frolicking in it, like hogs in mud.

"Anyway, suffice it to stay it's…memorable." He leaned forward and tapped the screen. The footage started rolling again. "Verndari sure make 'em big though, don't they?"

"Yeah…I'm learning that." She watched a veritable parade of them go in and out of the room as they met with various US dignitaries. Big-built and not a one of them under six feet plus.

"Wait is that–?"

"Senator Sapien," they both said in unison. A recent appointment to the Upper House after his predecessor unexpectedly vacated that seat. He walked in and began shaking hands with a line of six defenders. As he greeted them one by one, he smiled politely nodded and they exchanged words for a time.

"Too bad we couldn't get audio with this. I'd pay good money to hear what they're saying."

"For real." She did a web search on the senator for a couple minutes. "You're not gonna believe this." She flipped a few screens on the table in front of her. "Says here he's vigorously opposing a bill that's being piloted to push forward with implanted chip technology for all commercial transactions." She read verbatim from the news report– "It will eventually render all other forms of legal tender, cheques, swipe cards, even bitcoin and the like, unlawful and obsolete. If the Bill passes the House floor, voluntary trials involving thousands of US citizens will begin…within a year…" She looked up at Wright. "Okay, so that's like some real, next level–"

"Of biblical proportions…" Wright looked like he'd just seen a ghost. "Dear God… Didn't think I'd see it in my lifetime," he spoke almost to himself.

"Oh, wow. Check this out." She drew his attention to the screen and dialed the motion wheel back a few frames.

The senator was being escorted out by one of the defenders. They shook hands at the door for almost twenty seconds before he made a hasty exit.

"You see that?" He pointed.

"Yeah, that was a hella-long handshake, and he does not look happy about it."

"That's an understatement I'd say. I know the signs of someone being threatened."

In the next scene the defender who engaged in the long goodbye walked over to a decorative full-length mirror on the opposite side of the room, while the other five watched. He stood for a moment then he got eclipsed by a series of weird bright flashes.

When next he came into clear view it was no longer him standing there. It was Senator Sapien.

"No way!" She jumped up out of her seat unable to believe her eyes.

"That's some kind of glitch in the footage, right?" Wright leaned forward and squinted at the screen.

She dropped back into her seat, rewound it and played it again.

"Just what I was afraid of." He rose from his chair and started his customary pacing, "Our rogue defender from that murder case with…what did they call it, 'special powers'? He wasn't just an aberration. He's one of God alone knows how many others. So, not only can they take over a body, they can also morph into one of us. Did your GQ-holo defender tell you about this?" He stopped and put his palms down on the table.

"Not a word. And just for the record, he may be hella-tasty, but he's not *my* anything, Detective."

He gave her an odd look, then he smiled and shook his head.

He looked back at the screen for a long second.

"Well, wouldn't you think this is some critical info that he should have disclosed? I dunno, Monzo. Are you sure you can trust this guy?"

"Yes. Don't ask me how I know. I just do. Truthfully, I don't think I was in the frame of mind to get this kind of revelation, along with all he shared that day about hosting, and the Verndari weapons, and everything. I think that somehow…he knew that." She paused as she reflected on the personal connection they'd shared, in such a short space of time.

"Plus, I think he knew he'd be passing this along pretty soon anyway."

He ruffled his hair as he ran both hands through it at the same time. "Let me see it one more time."

She nodded and set it up to play again. As they watched she started thinking about how familiar those flashes of light were. Bright white but with an eerie reddish aura. She'd seen that before. But where? Then, it hit her, it was when she chased that defender in New Atlantis, and instead of catching him around the corner, she wound up scaring a young girl instead. But maybe what had sounded like fear to her was in fact an attempt to alter a voice pattern in a hurry.

Could it be…?

"Monzo!"

"Huh?' Her gaze snapped to Wright's bright blue one.

"Where were you just now?"

"Oh, my bad, just remembering something that happened back when I was with the NAPD, and wondering if the perp was one of these…shapeshifters."

"You know, I gotta say, you never struck me as the type to appreciate, or even know a song like that."

"Huh?"

"That tune you've been humming all morning when you're lost in thought. It's a popular church hymn called 'Great is thy faithfulness'."

"Really? It's been stuck in my head ever since last night. I didn't even realize I was humming it."

"Is that right?" He swiveled his chair around to

face her, eyes opening wide, he looked like someone switched on a light in his head. "And what happened last night to drive you to sing a hymn? You strike me as more of the type to be driven to drink." He gave a deep chuckle.

"And you would not be wrong." She pointed a finger at him and had a wry laugh at herself. "Well, a long time ago, anyway. I went through a real angry phase when my mom abandoned us. Long story for another time." She waved away the look of concern she saw on his face.

"Anything else you'd care to share?" His voice took on a softer tone. "This is a safe space. Whatever you say will never leave this room and I promise, you will be the better for it."

"Wow…that's like the second time I've heard that in as many weeks." She shook her head.

Not sure she was ready to share full details of her recent encounters with stone deities, spiral restraints and flies, but still not wanting to ignore the signs that she needed to find answers to what was likely a supernatural problem, she settled on a less complicated, softer cry for help.

She took a deep breath.

"So, what would you say if I told you I'm thinking about taking up my walk of faith again…from where I left off…when my husband died."

"I'd say…anyplace is a really good place to start. And by His grace, I'm just the person to guide you." He placed a comforting hand on her shoulder. "And now what would *you* say, if I say I'd like us to start with a prayer?"

"I'd say, lead on, Pastor."

They shared a smile, and then bowed their heads.

Chapter 9

Genesis 21:6
And Sarah said, God hath made me to laugh, so that all
that hear will laugh with me...

He glanced across at her, then looked away.

She took a sip from her coffee cup, then stared at him over the rim, waiting for him to look at her again.

He glanced up, did a double take, then held her gaze. She wiggled her eyebrows and grinned as she put the cup down.

His left eyebrow approached his hairline.

"No, not again." He groaned.

"Aw yeah." She nodded as they sat having morning coffee in an outdoor café. Or rather, as she sat having coffee. Other than a glass of club soda once, she didn't think she'd ever seen him eat, or drink anything, in the weeks since she'd met him. "Yep. I've def got your number today, Svik."

"I seriously doubt that, but go on ahead, Detective, by all means, have at it if you must. Let's just get it over with, so we can get down to business, shall we?" He put down the screen he'd been scanning for something he wanted to show her, looked directly at her and opened his hands in a gesture that signaled he was waiting.

"Okay, so the other day, I was wondering why a baseball I was looking at kept getting bigger and bigger…and then…it hit me!

"Oh, oh! Why can't you trust an atom?" He rotated his forefinger in a gesture that indicated he wanted her to speed up. "Because…they *make up* literally everything. Get it!

"Or wait, how about I was going to tell you a time travelling joke today, but I remembered, I already know you didn't like it.

"Aw, come on, seriously?" She threw her head back and roared as he shook his head at her. "Those were three of the best ones I read today. You really didn't find any of those just a little bit funny?"

His eyebrows rose and once again, she felt the customary, parental-like glare of his intense blue gaze.

"The very fate of humanity may well rest upon our actions over the coming months, Detective. Tell me, given the sheer gravity of that responsibility, do you really consider attempting to educate me in the finer points of your sense of humor, *and* getting me to join you in your mirth, to be a productive use of our time?"

She gave his weighty words some thought.

"And I say…hehll yes, Svik! Who gives a bad-devil-damn about living if you can't even have a laugh once in a while."

Undaunted, she reached over, slapped him on his arm and grinned wide. "You need to loosen up, I'm telling you. Work related stress is a leading killer of humans and prob'ly aliens too, in our age group."

She nodded.

He sighed and gave her a now familiar look. "Well, you're nothing if not consistent."

"Hey, I'll take that."

Smiling wide, she held out her hands and shrugged, as he sighed again.

Chapter 10

Leviticus 26:39
And they that are left of you shall pine away in their
iniquity in your enemies' lands...

"Actually, other than the more obvious and clear recommendations, like the one I got about praying and reading the Word that first night, some of the other stuff has just been straight up whack."

To advance her faith walk, Dani started meeting with Detective Wright in one of the precinct conference rooms at least twice a week, after they went off shift, and also after they discussed any updates on her meetings with Svikari.

On one particular night, about two weeks in, she felt comfortable enough to share some of what started her on her journey, as well as some of the more unusual events.

"I mean just the other night I'm sitting in this really nice Italian restaurant that my husband Joe and I used to like to go to whenever we caught the express sky-shuttle to Manhattan. Best food in the city by the way. Haven't been able to bring myself to go back there since he died, but you should try it. Anyway, the next thing I know, it's like we've stepped into one of those 21st century sitcoms." She caught his incredulous look. "I promise you I'm not kidding. For several minutes straight, or at least I think it was minutes. Time passes really different there." She shook her head. "So, anyway, literally every time I said something even slightly funny to Joe, an entire section at the back of the restaurant would light up, like it was under a giant spotlight and illuminate maybe fifty or sixty people just sitting like people used to do, you know, like in a studio audience and they'd just start laughing their heads off for a while, then they quit it and it went all dark again." She paused, waiting for his insights.

Detective Wright's expression was blank, at least until he started laughing. Really hard.

"Good one, Monzo, you almost had me for a minute there." He put a hand to his chest as he quieted.

"I am not messing with you, Detective. I'm dead serious. So come on, help me out here. What do you think it means?"

"I think it means you can hang with my girlfriend Alrissa, any time, is what I think, because the two of you watch way too much of that old time TV."

"Oh, but it's the best though, isn't it." She grabbed his arm.

"Yeah, it kinda is." He gave a wry chuckle.

"That 21st century entertainment was so much better than what we have now. There's no more Sci-Fi ever since the defenders got here. No more scripted dramas, or comedies, thanks to endless streaming reality TV and movies. Now everybody wants to share every detail of their lives on their individual broadcasting systems, no matter how personal, or hateful, or just plain pathetic it is. Just a constant parade of egomaniacs and thrill-seeking junkies trying to out-do each other for clicks and likes. I mean just imagine, all the celebs at all the award shows now are just average Joes like you and me, only lucky enough to get their five minutes of fame. It's hella-ridiculous when you think about it."

"Yeah. That it is." He shook his head on a grin. "So back to your night travels, anything else happen that didn't involve spectators?"

"Well," she paused, wondering how much she should share. "Sometimes things turn a bit dark, and I find myself in strange places that I wish I could escape in a real hurry. I'm not sure, but I think I saw an evil entity once. I just found myself in this crowded place. Looked like the underground in grand central station. He was standing off at a distance, when he spotted me. Really zeroed in on me, past all the other people, you know, like he immediately knew I wasn't one of them and didn't belong there."

Wright nodded.

"One minute he was meters away, and the next thing I knew, he was right in front of me. Started jabbing at me with needles…or something."

"What?!" Wright sat up a bit in his chair, looking alarmed.

"I dunno what it was, I just remember the pain being really isolated and sharp, and I recalled it clearly because…and this is the really weird part, normally, no matter what they come at me with, I'm blessedly numb. Barely feel a thing."

"Sounds like you must have a guardian angel out there somewhere, Monzo." Wright shook his head; his gaze still concerned.

"Maybe." She shrugged. "Anyway, it all felt so real, as real as you looking at me, and as close to me as you are right now. In the moment, I think I knew exactly what he was, yuh know? One of the fallen angels, and I just felt this total sadness come over me. It was strange. I should have been angry at him for what he was doing, but instead I just felt such pity. He must have noticed I wasn't trying to move my hands, or get away anymore, because he just stopped all of a sudden and looked directly into my eyes, and all I could think to say was…"

"I'm so sorry this happened to you."

"What?!" His tone was sharp and he stepped back a pace.

"I mean the fall. Why'd you even do it? Why'd you choose to leave *Him*," she referred to her Creator.

He didn't answer. Just shuffled his feet a bit and glanced around him with an anxious look on his face.

A face that kept changing.

Like he was suddenly struggling to maintain a solid form, his appearance melted and reformed over and over, morphing into someone different every couple seconds. Males as well as females, and of different ethnicities. It was unnerving to say the least.

And so very, very sad because she knew exactly what it meant.

It meant…he didn't even know who he was anymore because he'd just completely lost his identity.

An identity that had been originally, deeply and blessedly rooted…in the Creator…and was now…no more.

"How could you ever leave Him, for this?" She opened her arms wide to encompass their dark and dreary surroundings. People milled around, passing by them now and again with no real purpose, like they were all busy, doing nothing.

"Didn't you know what could happen? How can you even stand it?" She felt like she couldn't breathe for a moment, her eyes filling with sudden tears on his behalf.

She thought of her own experience of being forcibly separated from her husband, the love of her earthly life. And given how devastating that was, she couldn't even conceive of the kind of crushing despair he should be experiencing, being separated from the very author and fount of supreme love. To say nothing of the unending self-loathing, she imagined came with the fact, that it was by his own choice.

"Don't you miss Him?"

He glanced at her, then looked away.

"Sometimes…at Christmas time," he mumbled, "when so many of you remember… That you should remember Him…"

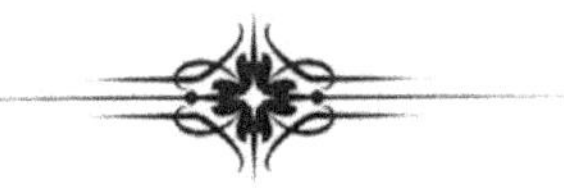

"He hustled away then, and I never saw him again." She shook her head.

Wright blinked away the wetness she noticed in his eyes.

"You know at first, he had me fooled. I thought, wow, that's such a revelation and so real. But he was lying."

"Why would you say that?" Wright looked crushed and confused.

"I could see it in his eyes, when he first glanced at me. He never looked me in the eye after that, and I knew what the real truth was. Because…it's what my answer would have been if the roles were reversed, and he'd asked me about Joe. I'd say yes, I miss him… Every. Nano. Second…" her lips trembled, even as she compressed them, "of Every. Single. Day. I think of him." She choked back a sob, as she tried to maintain control, and he reached out and grasped her hand that was closest to him. She gave a vigorous nod of her head as he held her hand between both of his, and as she met his deeply concerned blue gaze for a long second.

"You, okay?"

She nodded and took a deep cleansing breath, as he released her hand.

"Come to think of it now…strange, I didn't see her *that* time," she said to herself and sniffed.

"Who's this now?"

"Oh, didn't realize I said that out loud." She waved away her comment. "Yeah, I probably didn't mention, there's this young woman, a brunette, can't ever see her very clearly, but she's there sometimes too. She seems really bright and quirky. I tell you that girl is a Godsend. She's helped me out quite a few times. When I'm in danger like that. That's normally when I see her."

"Oh yeah? What's her name?" He looked at her with a curious expression on his face

"No clue. I just call her Superwoman because of the way she just takes to the sky and flies. You know I should be scared, every time I see her getting the hell outta Dodge, fleeing for her life like that." She smiled, and he chuckled. "But instead, it gives me hope."

"How so?"

"Because if a person can fly like that through Dante's nine circles of hell. Well, just imagine how incredibly amazing heaven will be."

"Wow, that's real, Monzo."

They shared a smile.

Her wristwatch alert went off, with no video.

"Hey, Svik, what's up?" She held up a finger to indicate to Wright that she needed a minute.

"Good evening, Detective. Can you meet me at the Kings Hotel in say an hour?"

"Sure. But isn't there like a big society, charity to-do on at the hotel tonight?"

Wright gestured and mouthed, "What?"

She shrugged and held out an open palm, to indicate she didn't know.

"Yes. I'll explain when you get here." Svikari's

voice gave nothing away. "I'll leave your name at the door."

"Okay. I'm on my way."

Chapter 11

Ecclesiastes 8:8
There is no man that hath power over the spirit to retain
the spirit; neither hath he power in the day of death: and
there is no discharge in that war; neither shall
wickedness deliver those that are given to it...

In less than an hour of receiving Svikari's urgent summons, Dani pulled up at the Manhattan hotspot where the star-studded charity event being hosted by a close friend of Senator Sapien's wife was being held.

She spoke her name at the door, and the AI allowed her entry into the grand hotel.

The Kings venue was a popular and very trendy five-star hotel, and tonight it was packed to the gills with guests dressed to impress at the night's event. She'd dismissed the thought of getting all pretty in favor of a timely arrival. But now she wondered if she should have at least gone home to change. Well, it's too late now. Tugging on the ends of her blazer, she stuck out her chest, tossed her head to make her curls bounce on her shoulders, and prepared to strut as she entered one of the huge ballrooms.

Impeccably dressed and standing out from the

crowd as Svikari tended to do, it wasn't long before she spotted him. His unmistakably gorgeous head of blond hair shining like a beacon across the brightly lit space.

"Okay, so I'm here, Svik." She reached up and tapped him on the back of his shoulder as she came up behind him. "What's the plan?"

He spun on his heel.

"Good evening, Danielle. How nice to see you again. Please, allow me to get you a drink." He turned back to the stunning red head standing beside him. "A pleasure to meet you. Excuse us, won't you Ginger?" Not waiting for his new friend's response, he placed a firm hand to her back and guided her in the direction of the holo-bar.

"A pleasure?" She snorted. "You don't even know what that means, do yuh?" She grinned. "And Ginger? Seriously? So, where's Candy, Cookie and the other female food groups tonight?" She held up the back of her hand to her mouth as she burst out laughing.

"Can you not dispense with the levity and be serious for just one evening?" His voice was mild as he glanced her way and kept propelling her forward.

"Of course. Of course. I gotta say though," she sobered. "I kinda like the way you said my name back there. I do believe that's the very first time you've ever called me by my given name." He looked down at her as they continued walking. "Say it again." She looked up at him and used her practiced sultry voice, just to get under his skin.

"Really, Detective? Haven't we covered this ground already?" His tone was matter-of-fact as he ushered her ahead of him through the doorway to the holo-bar. He chose a secluded corner booth and stood aside so she could slide in ahead of him. He sat opposite her as he signaled to a waiter.

"Oh, now this is *no-noice*." She looked around. Rubbed a hand over the plush seating, and admired all the fancy tech for gaming, gambling, private entertainment, and the like that she could see on the screens built into the surface of the table in front of them.

"What can I get for you sir." The stilted tones of the server android sounded cheery when he arrived at their booth.

"What's your pleasure?" Svikari looked to her for a response.

"Oh, nothing strong for me thanks, seeing as how I'm on the job and all." She made a show of winking at him.

He gave her a mildly exasperated look and turned to the waiter.

"Two club sodas, please."

Curious, she waited until the android moved away before questioning him.

"Well, yuh really do learn something every day. So, what's up with that, Svik? Are you like, a recovering alcoholic, or something?"

His left eyebrow shot up.

"You know, you're the second human female to ask me that. Why is that?" His tone was dry, but still carrying a note of genuine curiosity. "Is it really that uncommon for the males of your species to be teetotalers?"

"Tee-to-what-now?"

"Tee-totalers. It's a term for persons who eschew alcoholic beverages."

"Okay…so I'm not so sure I know what any of that means, but–"

"You know what…? I've changed my mind. I don't even want to know." He held up an open palm for her to stop, similar to what she'd done to him in the past. The most human gesture she'd ever seen him use.

"Don't look now, but I think I'm growing on you, Svik."

"You'd just love that wouldn't you?"

He shook his head as she nodded and smiled.

"For real though, why don't you ever laugh or even smile?" She softened her voice, wondering what life experiences were fueling that solemn expression he perpetually wore.

He closed his eyes, took a deep breath, and bent his head down to the table for a few long seconds.

If she didn't know better, she would have thought he was praying.

He looked up and pierced her with his blue regard.

"Where I come from, I'm…a warrior, with responsibility for many warriors and those placed under our protection. Fighting…for a world, continually at war. When the fate of those for whom you care deeply, rests solely and continually within your hands." He held his out on the table, palms up. "When the responsibility to succeed despite all odds, and against mounting opposition, from countless enemies, and even from those you're trying to protect and save. When that kind of weight rests entirely on your shoulders, well, there will only be time for jollity when the war is won…and everyone is home and safe. That's when we rejoice in victory. And oh…what a celebration it is…" A true smile briefly crossed his lips this time as his voice trailed off.

For long seconds after he spoke, he still held her gaze. And she saw it. Right there in the depth of expression in his eyes. Ageless and limitless wisdom, true integrity, humility, long-suffering and hard-fought self-control, innate goodness, love and…such joy in that small smile! Not the fleeting blush of transient happiness, but the everlasting gift of eternal and God-given joy.

She knew nothing of his planet and its political, or social structure, since the defenders had never shared such information with humanity. No one even knew where their planet was. Not even to which solar system it belonged.

She'd read news reports from when they first landed, claiming they would only say they wished to make a fresh start on earth, and didn't care to speak of the past. Some bulldog investigative reporters persisted but kept hitting the same brick wall. Getting the very same vague responses, like a prepared script they had all memorized, so eventually, everyone just quit asking.

If she wasn't sure before, now she was even more convinced he was different because she'd just got more from Svikari in one little conversation, than she'd ever seen or heard from any of the others in her adult life. And all of it was right there, shining out of his bright blue eyes, and through his perfect features.

She wondered why she'd never noticed it before,

as they sat in thoughtful silence until the waiter came back with their drinks. Svikari watched him leave then turned back to her, all business again.

"Okay, my human intel suggested otherwise, but the senator is here, tonight, in attendance with his wife. We may not get an opportunity like this again, so we should grasp it. One of them has already taken him as a host."

"What? But from the footage you gave me, I thought they'd try to replace him with one of their own."

"I suspect they may be wise to me. Or at the very least, aware that there's some type of a leak in their operation, so they've moved up their timeline. Successful shapeshifting is…difficult for them," he paused, like he was choosing his words carefully, "taking considerable time and effort. They have to watch their target, learn their habits, mannerisms, voice patterns and so on, to avoid exposure. Hosting is less complicated. Plus, I should mention that since here on earth, they are cut off from their true source, all Verndari have…a blemish if you will, that they simply can't hide or cover, even when they shapeshift, so that's how you'll recognize one of them, pretending to be human. It looks like this. See?" He put the palm of his right hand flat down on the table between them, and directly under one of the overhead lights that shone a bright spot onto that area of the table, while leaving the rest of the booth in cozy dimness.

She pulled on his fingers to lift the back of his hand off the table, and peered down at the mark. Just about an inch in diameter, it looked like a small circle with three smaller curls in it.

"They all have it." He pulled his hand back once she let go. "They pass it off as a birth mark if anyone asks."

She listened to everything he said, mulled over it, and then shared her first observation.

"Difficult…for them…hmm…" The investigative side of her brain, like a dog with a bone, latched onto his very first assertion and then kicked into high gear.

"Sorry?"

"The first thing you said. That shapeshifting is difficult for, 'them'." She raised her fingers and made air quotes as she repeated the last word.

"I think I've already established the dissimilarity between my former colleagues and me, as well as my wish to completely dissociate myself from them. I also believe I've used that particular pronoun numerous times in reference."

"Mm…no sir. Not like that you haven't." She shook her head at him. "The distinction you've drawn in the past has always been in relation to you not supporting their motivation and actions in progressing their agenda against mankind. That, just now, was more of a critique on an inherent capability. Suggesting that *they*, struggle with it. While *you*… don't."

For long seconds, she waited, hearing her heart thumping in her ears.

"It seems I may have underestimated you, Detective." The left side of his mouth quirked up in an attractive half smile as he looked at her with…admiration?

Something about his quiet note of confidence in her just then, touched her, but she still wanted a response.

"So?" She left the question open and waited.

"To what end, little one?" His voice turned soft seconds later. His gaze penetrating, as he looked across the table at her. "If you learn that I can, or can't, what then? I think I've already demonstrated that you can trust me. I also believe you know I'd never lie to you. Ask away. I'll answer. But given where we are in our journey, where *you* are in yours, and given the significance of all that we hope to achieve, are you really sure you need to know?"

This was another of the pivotal moments they'd shared since becoming acquainted. Like tonight, when he opened his heart to her, or that fateful morning she'd met him and was so touched by his compassion, his soul-searching gaze, coupled with the uncanny wisdom of his words.

"I will say this–if the answer to that question is yes…well then, you should get up and walk away right now." His voice and gaze were more somber than she'd ever heard or seen from him.

And she realized he was right. Either she trusted him, or she didn't. It was that simple. Everything else was just semantics at this point.

They regarded each other in silence for a long moment.

"Here, take this." He put his hand in his pocket then put it flat on the table and pushed something over to her. It was a small white pill in a plastic pack.

"It's a little something to help begin the process of extracting the senator's unwanted guest. Just get him to ingest it. I know who's inside, so if I'm really burned, he won't let me within a mile of him. He's…let's just say, not the brightest bulb in the bunch. He sees me coming, he's going to run fast and far. Whereas, you on the other hand…" His brows raised.

"Say no more. No going back. I got this, comrade."

"I know you do," he nodded.

Again, she felt such gratification. Didn't realize it until that exact moment, just how much his opinion of her mattered. Was that why she'd tried so hard to bring him a little joy with her humor? She'd thought it was for his benefit, but now she had to acknowledge that it had been for hers, just as much. That if she succeeded at just one of her several attempts to make him laugh, it would somehow impress him and make her worthy. Like a child seeking the attention of a parent, hanging on every little word of encouragement, when had she started performing for his approval? And what did that say about the state of her soul. She vowed to give it some prayerful thought.

"He hasn't spent more than ten minutes with his wife all night, and I've arranged for his secret service detail to be…indisposed for a while. Just be sure you get him to a private spot no more than five minutes after he swallows the pill."

"Say what?" She felt her heart and her face fall.

"You'll know why when you see it."

"Oh great! Because you know how much I just love a mystery, all wrapped up in a riddle." She twisted her hands around in a circle a couple of times.

"Thanks a lot, Svik. As if this wasn't already enough of a nut-buster."

"You got this, remember." His look spoke volumes.

She nodded.

She knew better than to ask him for full disclosure, or even a hint. She also knew he'd told her exactly what she needed to know, to see it done.

"Okay, I've booked one of the suites upstairs. Room 20075." He dipped into his pocket again and handed her a card key. "Just bring him directly to me when you're ready, and I'll do the rest. Off you go, and God speed, Detective."

She nodded, slid out of the booth. He watched her turn to leave.

"Jarit…" he said low.

"I'm on it, Michael." Her guardian popped in right beside her. "Don't give it another thought. I got this. They'll have to get through me to get to her." His expression was resolute and determined.

Michael nodded, then watched as Jarit turned with her, and they both headed to the exit.

Receiving a word from the Creator, he raised a hand and signaled to the server to bring him the bill.

Chapter 12

Job 18:5
Yea, the light of the wicked shall be put out, and the
spark of his fire shall not shine…

Dani left Svikari in the holo-bar and went in search of the senator.

The way she figured it, she could play it any one of three ways. Crazy, angry black woman with a vendetta. Crazy, angry black woman with a vengeance. Or, just plain crazy.

She turned a corner and spotted him on the right in the lobby. His right side to her, he was standing a short distance past the entrance to one of the hotel's ballrooms that was on the left, and he was completely engrossed with a larger than life 3-D holo of a seven foot plus, semi-nude woman. Every couple seconds, he waved his hand near her and the image changed, then she'd display some other part of her body from a different angle. And each time the rendering changed, he let out a weird little shriek of a laugh.

Sicko…

Dani recalled reading about the avant-garde artist who produced the work. And just like those 21st century pieces she'd seen in the museum of ancient and modern history, like the ten-foot square blank wall with a single blue dot at its center, she just didn't get it.

This particular artist had held a highly publicized showing a few months earlier. Like perverts at a very expensive peep show, some of New York's elite paid exorbitant amounts of money at an online bidding site to secure a spot at the packed event. All in an effort to procure one of the risqué works of art.

Beyond him was a dead end, with more questionable art pieces, and off to the right, closer to her than he was, she spotted a waiter, coming through a doorway. He started to cross the lobby looking like he was heading left towards the ballroom entrance, with a tray of an assortment of colorful drinks in hand. She stepped back a pace, put her back to the wall she'd just passed and shook the pill out of its package, as inspiration struck…

Crazy. It. Is…

She straightened her shoulders turned the corner again and strutted down the lobby to the waiter.

"Why, thank you." She grabbed up two small bright blue concoctions in shot glasses off his tray. He nodded, then she watched him enter the ballroom. She slipped the pill she had between the tips of her fingers into the one on the left and made a b-line straight across the lobby towards freak-boy.

"Well, good evening, Senator Sapien?"

He spun around as she drew near.

"Now, I thought that was you. How nice to see you here on this fine evening. I'm the very proud creator and spokesperson for this here…uh…blue blizzard. It's brand new on the market, and I cannot tell you what an honor it would be for you to give it just a big ol' ringing endorsement," she laughed just a bit too loudly, and pressed in on him to a degree she knew he'd find discomfiting.

He backed up a bit, looked at her and then at the drink with a confused expression on his face. "Uh…actually, I'm not–"

"Oh. No. No. No!" She gave him her best crazy, wide-eyed stare, and used her right forearm against his chest to push him through the 3-D woman and back almost to the wall behind him. She spilled a bit of both drinks in the process, but fortunately not nearly as much as she'd expected to, given her little maneuver. Satisfied that they'd now be well shielded from prying eyes, she advanced her little performance.

"Now, you know I will absolutely not take 'no' for an answer. You may not know this about me, but I have somewhere in the region of five *million* followers, most of them registered voters in the great state of New Atlantis, where I believe you're from?" She paused to let the number sink in. "And I know you would not be a happy camper, not in the least–," she cackled loudly again, "if I were to let them know I've discovered you have some type of difficulty with supporting young, bi-racial entrepreneurs…such as my good self."

She batted her eyelids at him to seal the deal, then held out the glass in her left hand

He hesitated, then accepted it.

"There we go, bless your heart. Now to get the full effect–" she glanced over her shoulder to ensure that only the holo was behind her, "– you've really got to take it all in at once. Just like a fine shot of Tequilla. So, here we go, all together, with me now."

She raised her glass in toast and smiled wide.

He did the same, though his smile was far from winning.

"Cin-cin!" She clinked her glass to his, pretended to lift it to her lips, then waited until his head was tilted back, before throwing the contents of hers, over her right shoulder.

He coughed and choked, turning beet red.

She thumped him on the back several times. "Has a bit of a kick, doesn't it? My bad. Did I not mention that? Takes some getting used to I know, but trust me…it's about to mess you the hell up." She barked out a laugh.

"Wha-aaa?" His speech sounded slurred, and she noticed his eyes becoming unfocused as he swayed towards her.

She gripped him by the arm, turned and pulled him back through the holo. Smiling at a couple guests who'd just emerged from the ballroom, she started walking him back the way she'd come.

"Now, why don't we find a nice, cozy spot, so I can tell you about how you can help with my distribution plan," she said loudly in case anyone was following their progress.

She got set to make small talk for the next five minutes.

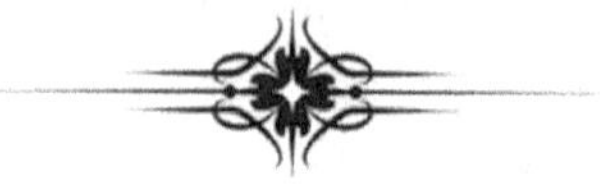

"Come on, come on. Just one more minute," she mumbled under her breath as she kept an eye on the time and a good grip on the senator's arm, as she hustled him towards the very furthest away in the bank of elevators.

"Uh… where am I?" His speech sounded really slurred now, and he leaned heavily against her.

"Just hang on, Senator, you'll be fine. Any minute now."

She prayed as she kept an eye on her surroundings, and on the very last elevator as the doors began to open.

Oh, thank the Lord…

A young stud. Perfect.

She looked down at her watch.

Time's up…

And right on cue, the senator, or rather his occupant began to writhe, hiss and spit.

Young stud on his way out of the elevator stepped back in, a look of abject terror crossing his features.

"Uh…now don't you be scared, sugar," she improvised on the fly and hissed right back at the senator a few times. "My hubby, he just gets so feisty when he starts role playing like this. We just need a little…uh…privacy, if you know what I mean?" She licked her lips. The senator kept twitching and hissing, his arm jerking in her tight grasp.

"Sure thing, sweet pea." Young stud winked at her, stepped out of the elevator and held out his arm against the edge to stop the doors from closing.

She paused, unprepared, as a wave of sadness washed over her. His use of a familiar endearment, stopped her cold for a moment, throwing her off her game. She blinked back sudden tears, took a shaky breath, recovered and pasted on a smile. In the next instant she pushed freak-boy hard, with a strength that surprised her, through the doors and up against the back wall. And like she was about to rock his freaky 'seven-foot-woman-loving' world. Looking back, she offered a sultry smirk to the young stud over her shoulder, as the elevator doors closed.

She blew out an anxious breath, stepped back, and wrestled her captive around to face her as she called out the floor. "Two hundredth." And, "Privacy mode," for an uninterrupted trip, so no one could get on board, before they got to their destination.

That done, she continued to battle with him for a couple more seconds, until she reached her breaking point.

Time for just plain crazy...part two.

Pressing her left fist hard up against his chest, to keep him against the wall, with her right hand, she reached to the back waistband of her trousers, under her blazer. She withdrew her weapon and pointed the barrel directly at the center of his forehead, with a steadiness she didn't know she was capable of, given the circumstances. He quit hissing, but kept on twitching every now and again, like an unattended water hose.

"Okay, so let's you and me game this out, shall

we? See, ordinarily I'd be betting that if I pull this trigger, both the senator in there *and* you, would quit breathing. But, given your *unusual talents*," she flicked her head to the side for a moment, then made a sucking sound with her left back teeth, "I just dunno. But yuh see, here's the kicker, even *if* you can somehow survive a bullet to the senator's brain, at point blank range. It's for damn sure, his body can't." She barked out a dry laugh.

"So, in that case, I'm willing to bet that your Verndari bosses won't be very happy with you for getting their prize horse in the coming election race. Shot. In the freakin' head." She snarled right in his face.

"And then, who knows," she softened her voice again, "maybe they end you themselves. Either way, I figure the odds of you living out the weekend don't look too good. Because, make no mistake, if you don't stop twitching like a damn crack addict… I will shoot you. Right here. Right now.

"So, what's it gonna be, *poo-boy*?" She leaned in again and eyed him. Hard. "You wanna test me right now, or do you wanna live?"

She released the safety on the gun.

Click.

He stopped moving, got deathly still.

"Yeah, that's what I thought." She tilted her head to the side to ease a sudden crick in her neck. She felt a rare warmth on the spot, and across her shoulders. Feeling a whole lot better all of a sudden, she reset the safety and tucked her gun back under her jacket.

"Poo-boy! Now even *you* have to admit that was just hilarious." Jarit roared with laughter, as he simultaneously massaged the soreness from Dani's neck, and addressed the Senator's unwanted possessor.

Then he got serious, channeled her inner crazy, and glared at the exile like he was set to rain holy fire down from heaven.

It retreated completely, allowing the still unconscious senator to come back to the forefront.

"We did it Dani." He would have high-fived her then if only he could.

"My girl!"

He barked out another laugh instead.

"That's right, here we go. Not in control of anyone now, are yuh?" she spoke under her breath for his ears only as she led him out of the elevator and down the corridor to the room in which Svikari awaited them.

She used the key and the door slid open to reveal a well-appointed living room, and Svikari, standing in the very center, as though he knew the exact time she'd get there. Hands loosely clasped in front of him, he strode forward.

"Thank you, Detective. Your assistance has been invaluable, to say the least."

"Sure," she nodded.

The Kings Hotel was one of just three of the highest structures in New York at the time, and never having been this high up before, she was curious. She left him and the senator, and walked over to the glass wall, and its shimmering energy shield directly ahead.

"Wow." She stopped about three feet away from it, looked down at the lower Manhattan skyline, far below, across at a couple low clouds floating by, and then up, at the full moon and stars so close she felt she could reach out and touch the very heavens.

She turned and walked back over to where Svikari stood waiting.

"That's quite a view you've got there. Guess you're not afraid of heights. How can you stand to be this high up? I thought I might get a nosebleed in the elevator on the way up."

"I like it." He shrugged. "It reminds me of where I come from."

"Must be an amazing place." She glanced back at the view.

"That it is."

He said it with such sincerity and that innate joy again, that she'd sensed in him in the holo-bar, she felt his intense connection to his home all over again.

"Sounds like something I'd wanna see. Maybe I will, one day?" She said almost to herself as she looked up into his captivating eyes.

"You most definitely will, Danielle." He

nodded, looked down at her, and held her gaze.

It was such an odd thing to say, given how far away his planet must have been. A near impossibility really. Maybe it was just the way he said it, or the fact he said her first name again. She didn't even really know why, but she believed him.

She broke their eye contact and looked over at the senator, remembering why they were here, in this magical suite in the sky.

"By the way, what the hell was in that mickey you had me put in his drink? First, the real senator seemed to make a return appearance, then next thing I knew he was twitching, and spitting and hissing like a snake. Now, it's like he's off to Zombieland." She tugged on his arm and eyes staring straight ahead he made not a sound, but obediently took a step forward.

"You're better off not knowing, trust me."

"Uh-huh." She eyed him. "So, what now?"

"Now, I evict an unwanted squatter and allow the senator to get back to his life and his family. He won't remember a thing."

"And is *that* something I'd wanna see?"

He gave her a pointed look that spoke volumes given their past association and recent experience.

"Yeah...that's what I figured." She tapped a booted foot on the floor and shook her head. "What can I say? It's been real. See you when I see you, Svik." She handed him the room key she'd used, turned on her heel and gave him a peace-out sign over her shoulder, as she sashayed to the door and exited the room.

The door slid closed behind her with a soft whistle.

In the circumstances, given their victory, Michael allowed himself a slight smile at her trademark humor. Then, in an instant he transformed into his true self.

He allowed his light to flow, out from his heart, and down his right arm. Then he curved his fingers, plunged them into Senator Sapien's throat, and pulled.

Temporarily unconscious, the senator fell to the floor.

His evil possessor did not.

It took a minute for his vile usurper to fight its way back to consciousness. As he watched, its eyes finally opened and then grew wide with obvious fear as it focused on him with full knowledge, recall and recognition.

"I don't suppose you'd care to repent, like Andeo did?" His hand pulsed with blindingly brilliant white light as he kept a firm grip on its neck.

"We are Legion," it sneered in the old tongue.

"Not anymore," he said in English, then watched with grim satisfaction as it disintegrated into cosmic dust, within his grasp.

Chapter 13

Song of Solomon 1:2
Let him kiss me with the kisses of his mouth: for thy love is better than wine…

"Just leave them, sweet pea. I'll clean up."

They just had some friends over for dinner, and after giving her a soft kiss, Joe waved away her offer of help as he moved the dishes from the table to the kitchen counter himself. He started loading the dishwasher.

"Hmm, sweet pea, huh…? That's different."

"What?" He glanced up, then went back to his task.

"I just noticed that since we got married last month, every now and again you call me sweet pea. I don't remember you ever calling me that before, when we were going out. It's cute."

"Uh-huh." A secret little smile played around his lips.

"There," she pointed at him. "What, was that?"

"What was what?" He opened his eyes wide. Tried to look all innocent, but she knew better.

"Oh, you know exactly what. Come on, Doc. You know I am the queen of micro expressions, so spill it. Don't make me go all gangster up in here." She pointed around the kitchen that was his sole domain. He liked everything just so, and would practically get a heart attack, if she so much as moved a bottle of spices to the wrong shelf.

He chuckled but didn't fess up as he made another trip to transfer items from the table to the counter.

"Oh, I know… Is dem Caribbean stewed pigeon peas I makin' now dat yuh like so much, eh?" She tried to imitate her cousin's Trinidadian accent.

His laughter rumbled all around her as he shook his head.

"Sorry to break it to you, babe, but your cousin's stewed *everything*, tastes a whole lot better than yours. Hey! Hey!" He grinned as he successfully dodged the fake one-two punches, she directed at his arm. "And that accent sucks, by the way."

"Yeah, I know. Gimme a break here, I'm working on it."

"Which one? The peas, or the accent?" He grinned again.

"Both." She barked out a laugh.

"Okay so if it's not that, then…aww…I know. Is it something that your grandad called your nonna? How sweet?" She knew what a major role the charming, hardworking, elderly Italian couple had played in his upbringing, and how much he loved and admired them.

"Nope and give it up, because there's nothing to tell." He bent to put a couple more plates in the dishwasher.

"The hell there ain't."

Inspiration struck, and she tried a different tack.

"I bet I can make it worth your while… if I…" her tone turned musical as she bent and whispered into his ear.

He raised up, his reddening face snapping around so sharply she thought he might get whiplash

"Really? You'd do that?"

She tiptoed as far as she could, reached up and buried her fingers in his soft, thick mane, and then pulled his head down to her, "Uh-huh," and punctuated each sound with a single soft kiss to his lips.

She started to pull away, but he grasped her by the waist, bent his head and subjected her mouth to a much deeper and more thorough tasting.

"Okay." His sweet surrender was a manly growl against her lips. Even as she purred in triumphant response.

"So, the sweet part…well that's just obvious. 'Cause I sure can't get enough of all this here tasty, and luscious, brown sugar."

She giggled as he dropped his head to lick and nibble at her neck.

"But what you're probably missing…is the second bit," he kissed his way up to her ear, "because, it's not so much a word–" he spoke at her ear, his voice a grating rumble, "–as it is, a letter."

He looked into her eyes then, tilted his head a bit, and lifted his left brow.

His smile, feral.

She let out a little shriek, as much from the realization of what he meant, as from his next action, as with a wave of his hand he swept the last of the dishes aside.

Lifting her, he joined their mouths in a hot, sweet tangle, even before he'd hoisted her up to their kitchen counter.

"Playtime's over?" she breathed against his lips.

He bit down gently on hers. Soothed the sweet nibble with a brush of his tongue.

"Aw yeah… Playtime's definitely over."

Chapter 14

1 Corinthians 15:55
O death, where is thy sting? O grave, where is thy
victory?

"All units be advised, we have a credible, I repeat, a credible bomb threat at the summit of world leaders at the International Diplomatic Center. Please respond."

"Ten-four. This is Unit 19 responding. I'm just about ten minutes out," Dani answered the precinct AI's call.

She flipped on her siren and lights, checked her rearview then slammed on the brakes. Swinging the car around and onto the east bound lane, she floored the gas as she headed back in the direction from which she'd just come.

Out front of the Center was complete chaos when she arrived.

She jumped out of her car. "Hey!" She held up her badge as she called out to a uniformed officer, "Get these people back!" She pointed to indicate the dozens of pedestrians, media personnel, and looky-loos milling around on the wide pavement that bordered the entrance to the center.

"And clear a two-block perimeter from here to Main. Now, officer!" she shouted to get him moving.

"Yes, Detective, right away." He signaled to a couple of his fellow officers and started to do her bidding.

Satisfied, she turned towards the entrance and started walking quickly towards it.

"Officer! Officer! Marly Sparks with K and C Media. Can you confirm, or deny, there's a serious threat to the President at today's summit?"

"No comment." She issued the automatic response without looking back at the reporter who was trying, but not succeeding, to keep pace with her.

"Officer, please… I need this scoop. This is the opportunity of a lifetime for me. My opportunity to climb out of the dismal and miry trench of invisibility at my media house."

What the hell kinda reporter says stuff like that?

Intrigued, Dani stopped. "I said, no comment, and it's Detective–" she spun around, "–not offi–" She froze, unable to finish her reprimand.

She knew those wide green eyes, the chic brown hair, and the attractive face previously indistinct, but now brought into sharp focus.

"Oh, my God. It's you," they said in unison.

"Superwoman? You're real?"

"Well, of course, I'm real. After all those creepy night travelers we escaped. What? Did you think you were dreaming?"

"Hell yeah, what else would anybody in their right mind think."

They stared at each other for a moment more, then screamed as they came together in a big warm hug.

"I can't believe it's really you." Marly held on tighter as she rocked them both from side to side.

As gently as she could, Dani extricated herself. "Look… Marly? Is it?"

She nodded.

"I hate to break up our little reunion, but I've got a job to do in there," she pointed to the Center.

"Of course, of course, offic–uh… Detective…"

"Danielle Almonzo."

"Right. Danielle Almonzo. Got it!" She smiled.

Dani turned to leave.

"Wait, Detective? What about that scoop?"

She turned back, "You'll be the first one I take questions from when we do the secondary news briefing later. How's that?"

"Yes!" Marly pumped a fist in the air.

Dani shook her head on a laugh, then turned and sprinted towards the Center's entrance.

The entire building was on lockdown, so she held up her badge to the scanner at the door and stepped inside as soon as the doors slid open. Once inside, she spotted a couple of her fellow brothers in blue, among them a Detective she knew fairly well from another precinct, talking with some in-house security officers at a reception desk off to the left. On the right, just a short distance from the entrance, the small group of reporters, representing the media houses that won that day's broadcasting lottery were gathered. The lottery entitled them to be on site, front and center, for any developing, newsworthy events such as the bomb threat currently underway at the international summit.

The primary news briefing, once everything unfolded, would be done solely for the benefit of this group inside the venue, giving them a golden opportunity to increase their notoriety and viewership exponentially. There was a minimal energy barrier that could be turned on to shield them should things go sideways, but they were still putting themselves at great risk just by being there. Due to the obvious danger to them, they were each required to sign a waiver absolving the relevant authorities of any responsibility should their actions, or mere presence, compromise their personal safety in any way. Thanks to the upsurge in demand for more edgy realism in reporting, news agencies were getting more and more brazen and reckless in their attempts to wow their followers.

Danielle shook her head as she took in each of their eager faces. She wondered if their avaricious corporate financiers, and attention-starved viewers, would even care about the personal cost to them and their families should things go south. She was willing to bet not a one of them had really considered that they could quite literally get blown to bits that very day, live on the news at noon.

Unbelievable…

Ignoring their calls to her for a comment as she passed them, she headed for the group huddled at the reception desk. But before she could get there, a tall, good-looking guy, dark hair, medium build separated from the press group and got to her in three long strides. He stuck his wrist cam nearly in her face, forcing her to halt her progress.

"Detective, good morning, Dax Newton – Earth

Network News." His voice was like velvet covered gravel. Perfect for his chosen profession. Smooth and cultured, but with a deep throaty undertone. She might have found it, and him, appealing if he wasn't currently being such a pain in her butt.

"Any initial insights on this morning's events you'd care to share with our viewers?"

"No comment." She tried to move past him, but he blocked her path still holding up his wrist near her face.

"Detective, sources inside, on the ground, say there may be more than one explosive device on the premises. Can you say if anyone else other than the president is an intended target?"

"Man…which part of 'no comment' didn't you get? Let me break it down for you. Real clear," she eyed him. "Clear. Like a shooting star, across the dark night sky. You better get that wrist cam out of my face, or you'll be picking it, and the pieces of your busted hand, up off the floor. And then, I'm gonna arrest your sorry butt for obstruction."

He got a confused expression on his face, then his eyes opened wide. He looked at her like he'd just seen a ghost.

She gave him one last glare, walked around him, and continued to the reception desk.

"Detective, wait, just give me one minute, please!"

She heard him calling out behind her, but she ignored him and stepped into the electronic privacy space. It was set up to keep conversations going on at the reception desk from reaching the press group, until they were ready to address them with an official statement. Like a cone of silence, it was semi-circular at the bottom, extending all the way back to the bank of elevators behind them, but then it narrowed to a peak at the top.

"Gentlemen, Detective Almonzo of the 15th." She held up her badge. "What have we got?"

"Hey Monzo. It's been a minute."

"Rigsby." She nodded and gave a slight smile, as she shook hands with the officer from the 80th.

"Barton. Head of the Center's security." The guy standing next to Rigsby stretched out his hand, and she shook it. "The word about a bomb came in at oh-eleven hundred. We put in the call to police dispatch and the bomb squad shortly after that. Said they're about thirty minutes out, given midtown land and air traffic."

"Okay, so how quickly can we evacuate POTUS and the other summit delegates?" Rigsby got the discussion going.

"Secret service thinks it's a hoax." Barton shrugged. "Still, we swept their floor, two above and two below and they're clear. I'm told the discussions are at a very sensitive stage and due to the importance of the summit, they've opted to carry on, but with ramped up shield protection of course, until we get confirmation. If it's legit, and a level red threat, we can move them all out to a safe distance within minutes. We're in constant contact with the secret service team. I've got my maintenance guys searching everywhere else, floor by floor."

"Okay good. In the meantime, let's have your team here check internal surveillance cams." Dani extended a hand to indicate the other two members of the Center's security team standing nearby. "You guys," she turned to the three uniformed police officers, "check the traffic cams around the Center for any suspicious activity and make a sweep of social media and the dark web, just in case there's any chatter." They nodded.

"Any special arrangements for the event today?" Rigsby addressed that question to Barton.

"Yeah, did you outsource any services for the Summit? Cleaning, servers, catering?" Dani caught Rigsby's train of thought and ran with it.

"Uh…yeah," Barton nodded. "We were told that some of the Defender delegates have very…ah…peculiar tastes, so we had to bring in a couple of their people to cater to their dietary requirements. Head chef and two others. They're set up down in the basement. Two levels down."

"The basement? What gives?" Alarm bells went off in Dani's head as she cocked it to the side.

I don't wanna get too much into it, but suffice it to say it's cause of the smell. Pretty nasty stuff they're putting together down there."

"Okay, so Rigsby?" She turned to her colleague.

"Don't look at me, Detective," he held up his hands, "I got a weak stomach and an even worse gag reflex. We might need the defenders help with this, and if I get so much as a whiff of what Barton's talking about, it's all over. I'm guessing projectile vomit all over their lunch won't go over too well with the aliens." He let out a dry chuckle.

"Really Rigsby? Did yuh just miss the defender sensitivity training all together? We never use the 'A' word, remember?"

He shrugged.

She sighed.

"All right, so you check the AI security logs to see if anyone got in without clearance, and I'll head down to the basement, I guess. Barton, you got any issues, or a delicate constitution like the princess over there?" She jabbed a thumb in Rigsby's direction and grinned.

"Oh, so you got jokes? That was cold, Monzo." Rigsby made like he was shivering in the wake of her comment.

Barton chuckled and shook his head.

"Okay, then I guess you're with me. We've got no idea what the timeline is here guys so let's work quick and smart." She looked to each of the seven men around her. "Keep your heads on a swivel, and your coms close. Let's do this. Lead the way, Barton."

She followed him to the elevators, and they quickly descended to the 2nd level basement.

It looked like they were using it for storage mostly. Three guys in maintenance uniforms were carefully sifting through boxes, crates, and furniture. They all looked up as she and Barton entered, but one stopped what he was doing, and came over to them.

"Anything yet?" Barton lifted his chin.

"Nothing yet, boss. We've just got one more level down of basement to cover then we'll join the rest of the guys searching the upper floors."

"Okay, keep at it."

"What's over there?" Dani pointed as she noticed a doorway to the left, past the piles of boxes and crates leading to another space.

"That's where the defenders are set up doing their thing."

"Okay, mind if I check it out?"

"No, be my guest. But don't be surprised if you don't get very far."

"Huh?"

"You'll see," he chuckled. "I'm headed up to the 9th. You gonna be okay on your own for a spell?"

"Yeah, sure."

"Just call on one of the guys here or use the coms if you need anything."

Okay, got it." She watched him get back into the elevator, then made her way through the obstacle course to get to the doorway. She got within only about six feet of the entrance to the mystery door, before it whistled and opened just enough to allow a big burly guy to step out. He crossed his arms over his massive chest and stood with legs braced apart in front of the door as it closed again.

She felt a wave of heat and got a whiff of something really vile. She held her breath for a second or two.

Barton wasn't kidding. It was like rotten eggs and something else…

"Good morning. NYPD." She stopped her advance and flashed her badge. "We've had a threat on the building. Just need you to step aside, so I can secure this area."

"No need, officer."

"It's Detective…and I'll be the judge of what's needed. Now stand aside and let me through."

"I'm afraid I can't allow that…for your own safety." He pierced her with an unusually shadowy gaze. Even from this distance she could see his eye color was so darkly intense; she couldn't distinguish the unusually large iris from the pupil.

"And how do you figure that?"

"The entire room has been retrofitted to operate in a manner that you would probably consider to be akin to an oven. Your body would not be able to tolerate the temperature." He smirked.

"Uh-huh…" She tapped her booted foot on the floor. "Well just for my own edification, why don't you open the door just a bit, so I can take a little look-see. If I stand over here, I'm pretty sure I'll be far enough away from any adverse effects."

He didn't move. And she waited. Counted in her head to stay calm…

One Mississippi, two Mississippi…three…

"Look." Angered by his stubbornness, she moved onto plan B. "There's only one way this ends, bro, and that's my way." She crossed her arms over her chest and took a step forward. "So, you can comply and open *that* door." She pointed, then put her hand on her taser. "Or, I can stun your ass, and get these guys to drag you outta my way. Your choice. What's it gonna be?"

His face turned nearly purple, a mask of barely leashed rage. He looked like he was about to challenge her again, but then he got kind of pale, his eyes not quite meeting hers.

"Very well." He waved a hand near the door, and it opened, less than a foot. He still didn't move.

She felt his glare burning a hole in her head as she leaned to the side, so she could see past his big body, and caught a glimpse of the room behind him.

Another two, who were standing at a doorway glowing bright red and smoky, and even further in, glanced back. They turned towards her, but then strangely spun back. The room closer to her was glowing a dimmer red and there was that awful egg smell again. She put a fist under her nose. It was like what she imagined hell smelt like... Like...

Burning sulfur?

Granted, she didn't know a thing about Verndari cuisine, but she'd bet her butt that whatever they were concocting in there wasn't for their consumption.

"I know it's near the south exit, but is that safe?" She looked up at the big guy. "A fire pit like that in the basement of a building like this?"

"Perfectly."

He said no more, and she was itching to challenge him, but other than the floor to ceiling gateway to Hades, she nearly snorted on a laugh, there was nothing else unusual that she could see. So, deciding that discretion was for sure the better part of valor, she stepped back and nodded. He turned, opened it just enough to go through and quickly disappeared again as it closed.

Before she turned to make her way back through the clutter to the elevators, she noticed one of the maintenance guys on the right, down a corridor she hadn't seen on the way in, eyeing her strangely. Something about his squirrelly movements and shifty look piqued her investigator's intuition, so she walked over to him instead.

"So, how's it going? How much longer before you guys finish this floor, you think?"

"Shouldn't be long now," he mumbled as he averted his gaze and lifted a crate he was going through. He moved it over to where she was, almost dropping it on her right foot.

"Hey, watch it man…damn!" She pulled her foot out of the way, just barely.

"Occupational hazard." He leered at her and reached down again to shift it a bit further to the right, and away from her feet. Looking down, she noticed the back of his hand, as he gripped the wooden box.

"Interesting tat you've got there." She recognized the coin shaped marking Svikari had showed her a couple weeks earlier.

His gaze flew up to hers.

"Where'd you get it?" She tilted her head to the side and narrowed her gaze on him. "…Vern…dari."

His face got red, and for just an instant, it changed. Like a micro expression, she might have missed, if she wasn't paying attention.

It was him.

But before she could even react, he rose up and pushed her. Hard. Sent her crashing into a pile of cardboard boxes and crates.

It was the same defender she'd chased through the streets of sector seven in New Atlantis. It had been five years, but she never forgot a face, and like Detective Wright always said, there were no coincidences. A bomb threat in the building, and he just happened to be there, with the Center's maintenance crew? It was almost a guarantee he was in on it, up to his no-good, Verndari, shape-shifter eyeballs.

She scrambled to right herself, winced as she felt a sharp pain in her hip and thigh. Standing with difficulty, she started limping after him, just barely taking note of the startled faces of Barton's maintenance guys beginning to react as they scrambled to get past the items in their way to get to her.

"Hey you, stop! NYPD! I said stop!" She shouted after the guy as he ran further down the corridor towards the emergency exit about fifty meters away. He kept running as though she hadn't even spoken, got to the exit and put his hand up to the sensor.

"Oh, hehll no, not again."

Taze him Dani… she heard in her head.

"Not this time, big-boy." She stopped, drew her laser-tagging taser and wasted no time in aiming it at his back. She fired.

She knew she hit him, but strangely, it seemed to take a second, or two. Then he just dropped, like a stone. His body completely still, with none of the jerking that should have accompanied the passage of some fifty thousand volts through his big body. Obviously Verndari physiology was vastly different from a human's.

"You, okay?" One of Barton's guys finally got to her.

"A whole lot better than that guy." She blew out a breath.

"I'll say. Nice shot, Detective." He grinned and nodded. "Who is he?"

"No clue, but trust and believe… I'm about to find out."

Thrilled that the Creator had allowed her to hear him that time. Jarit let his light recede from his left hand, back along his arm and into his heart, as he stood over the exile, or public enemy number one, as he'd referred to him earlier in Dani's journey.

Of course, she couldn't have known as he did, that the human weapon would never, could never, harm her intended target.

Her earthly weapons were carnal. Unlike Jarit himself, who was of Almighty God. Built for the pulling down of evil strong holds.

Just like this.

Knowing the Creator was satisfied with the outcome, in the blink of an eye, he returned to her side…

After she got checked out by Sky-Med, and they gave her something for the soreness in her leg, Dani rejoined Rigsby, Barton, and the security team. As it turned out, they found something unusual in the crates that the defender she arrested was going through. Figuring that he likely planted it there himself, she planned to conduct a little investigation of her own, before they hauled him off to the precinct. But remembering a promise she'd made; she gave Rigsby a few comments for her part of the primary briefing and headed out in search of Marly first. She spotted her on the pavement, exactly where she'd left her hours earlier. She was looking eagerly towards the entrance.

Now, this girl is a straight-up bloodhound...

She shook her head and grinned. Motioned her over as she crossed the pavement towards her.

Marly waved and started a swift approach, but then halted halfway there. She pointed; her eyes wide. "Detective, behind you!"

Dani spun around.

Oh God... Charlie Swift

Looking just as he had in that first freaky dream she had months earlier, except this time he was about twenty paces away, weapon already drawn and trained on her.

He smirked.

She reached for her own weapon, but too late.

She heard the loud explosions and felt the intense pain, and fell backwards, as she took two hits to the chest.

In and out of consciousness Dani fought to focus on Marly's anxious words.

"It's okay. You're okay. Come on, look at me Danielle. Please."

But it was getting harder and harder when, just behind her young friend, stood–

A glorious angel of light.

His awesome beauty was singular, unlike anything she could ever dream to imagine. She just couldn't bring herself to look away.

"Detective! You open your eyes and look at me, right now! You hear me?!"

Unlike the angel who looked serene and stoic, Marly sounded like she was in full panic. And with that, came a grim realization. She forced her eyes to open a crack and saw blood… everywhere.

"Oh God…have mercy on me…I'm dying, aren't I?" she grated out.

"No, no! You hold on. Sky-Medics will be here soon. Oh God, there's so much blood. Somebody, please help me!" Marly sounded frantic as she felt her hands press down on the wounds in her chest.

In complete contrast to Marly's frenzy, the look the angel gave her was filled with calm, yet intense compassion.

She felt her grip on reality slipping away. "Please…tell Joe…I love him…"

"Tell him yourself, little one…" Her angel finally spoke, as though from far away and he sounded just like–

Svikari?

Yep, she must be dying. And it wasn't that she was afraid of death or anything, she just really wanted to know why the H-E-and-two-sticks she needed to be here when it happened.

She saw her angel smile wide and it was stunning. A second later, and he burst into hearty laughter.

Def not Svik then…because he'd probably never laughed like that a day in his life. She fought to hold a thought, as his laughing face and everything around her receded and faded to black. Or maybe it was she who was being pulled away…

Feeling weightless she floated in a sea of such calm, and peaceful darkness she let it happen.

And just let go...

Chapter 15

Revelation 12:10
And I heard a loud voice saying in heaven, Now, is come
salvation, and strength, and the kingdom of our God,
and the power of His Christ: for the accuser of our
brethren is cast down, which accused them before our
God, day and night...

Flashes of light broke through the blackness.
As though summoned–faces, places, and things she
knew she'd done wrong rose all around her like dark
billowing smoke. Taunting her.

A voice spoke. Loud. Insulting. Jeering.
Accusing.
Until…one word–
"Enough."
Such a soft, yet strong–calm, yet commanding–
all powerful instruction,
And utter silence reigned.
Until…
"Father...she's one of mine."
And just like that. In an instant, she was
surrounded, embraced, and lifted by light, so much
light. Peace, warmth, and such ease enfolded her. In
a word–love. Amplified and tangible. Tears welled

up, bursting forth as she sobbed in relief, in joy and in deepest gratitude.

Her sobbing quieted and then ended, as she floated down in a cloud of complete comfort. The bright light behind her closed eyelids faded to a pale orange. She felt warmth, under her bare arm. Like wood heated by afternoon sun, and then simultaneously heard and felt the soft lapping of water, cool and refreshing.

She opened her eyes slowly, lifted her head off her arm, and looked down. The water splashing up between the planks of wood beneath her was the brightest, crystal-clear blue she'd ever seen. She looked much further down and brought countless iridescent grains of sand into focus. She marveled as each of them sparkled white, then clear, and then with all the colors of a beautiful rainbow. Through the layers of water her gaze rose again, to just below the surface where a pretty, little silver and red fish about the size of her fingernail swam up. Without thought she reached down and her breath caught, as her hand and arm passed right through the wood to the water beneath. The cool touch of the liquid sent a wave of intense pleasure surging through her, even as the fish looked up at her as it brushed up against her palm, and then swam playfully back and forth between her fingers, tickling her and making her giggle.

She pulled her hand back and looked around her then. She was on the dock at the back of her parents' summer home. She'd had many happy times there when she was a child. It looked as she remembered it, but then, it didn't. Every blemish and imperfection in the structure of the house and its surrounding backyard was gone. The sky was intensely blue and lit with gorgeous reds, oranges, and yellows in the sunlight. Further afield and in an instant, she could see every leaf on every tree, she zeroed in and could see every feature of the birds flying overhead, petals of incredibly beautiful flowers and varying shades of green of each blade of grass in the nearby woods. Her brain processed what she was seeing with unimaginable clarity, speed, and ease. And more than that, all seemed to be singing a melody of thanksgiving and praise that resonated at a level deep down in her spirit. She looked down at the exquisite wood grain of the dock again…and saw a hand.

"Hey, Dani."

"Joe?" She followed the hand up to his loving face. Perfect now, in its symmetry and appeal. The scar on his chin he'd got when they were children was gone. His forehead and cheeks, no longer marred by the ravages of earthly cares and time. His gray-blue eyes penetrating, brighter and more alive than she had ever seen them. The faint strands of silver that had tainted his dark mane–gone and replaced by a lustrous thick black that covered his head and brushed his shoulders in long, rich, sun-catching waves. He nodded and smiled as she took his hand, and he pulled her to her feet…and right into his arms. Her heart and spirit sang, in union with his, as their lips joined in a long, sweet kiss.

"I'm so sorry. I didn't keep my promise for so long." His wish to have her keep the faith sprang to her mind.

"It's okay, I know. It's all okay now. He makes

all things new." He brushed her curls back behind her ears and pressed multiple soft kisses to her face. His hug was fierce as he enfolded her in his arms again. "I love you so much."

"I love you more." She thought she might have cried her heart was so full. But instead, there was nothing but pure, undiluted joy, hers and his, that she could now feel as though it were all her own. Filling her to bursting and somehow joining with everything else around her. Suddenly overwhelmed, she felt lightheaded.

"Deep breaths. Come on, breathe with me." She mirrored him as he inhaled and exhaled slowly, as he peered down at her. "There you go." He smiled and cupped her cheek.

"Wow." The feeling receded to a pleasurable buzz, as she followed his lead and focused on his words and comforting touch.

"I know. Right?" He grinned. "It's the bliss. You'll get used to it."

"Uh-uh, bite your tongue. I don't ever wanna get used to that."

"There she is. There's my girl." He nodded and smiled.

She grinned, and they both laughed out loud as he lifted and swung her around and around, just like he had when they were teenagers.

"Okay, I think you're ready now. He's been so anxious to see you."

He pointed and she already knew before she even turned around.

He was sitting on the neat immaculate lawn at the back of the sprawling house, with a small child.

Pointing to a nearby tree, He held out His hand and a bird left its lofty perch and flew straight to Him. He caressed its proud chest and wings with such tenderness and care she felt her heart fill to bursting again.

She didn't know if she floated or flew, but at the speed of thought in a scant second, her feet touched down and she stood before Him.

He handed the beautiful bird to the child, and she laughed in sheer glee as she petted and played with it.

He stood then and Dani sank, to her knees before Him. Overcome with emotion, she hung her head. Touched the flesh of His sandalled feet, near the ragged holes, with gentle fingers.

In silence He pulled her up and enveloped her in a hug that felt like Christmas and springtime and new beginnings, all rolled into one, and in her spirit, she knew that no words would ever be necessary.

He sat down again, beckoned her to do the same as He touched the top of the little girl's head. About five years old, she released her pet to return to its tree, as His touch and loving smile had her opening her tiny arms for Him to take her into His embrace. He started to lift her and eager, she climbed into His lap and started to play with a long swath of His hair.

Dani knelt for the second time, until her gaze was in line with gray-blue eyes that were the very same as Joe's.

"Zoey…?"

"Mommy!" The tot's eyes lit with immediate recognition, and she launched herself into Dani's arms. She caught her to her chest.

"My baby!" She covered her face with butterfly kisses, pressed her lips to the top of her head, and inhaled the sweet fragrance of summer flowers, stirred by the mere touch to her hair. She pulled on Joe's hand, anxious to get him into their family hug, as he too knelt beside her. "Thank you, Lord." She let all her gratitude shine through as she spoke over the top of Zoey's tiny head.

He stood with inherent grace, placed the open palm of His right hand on the top of her head for a long second, and in her spirit, she heard–

"Never forget… My greatest joy, is fulfilled in you…"

She nodded, then looking back at Joe, she smiled.

He placed his hands on her arms and leaned in, touched his forehead to hers.

She closed her eyes and smiled.

Finally, she was home…

Chapter 16

Psalms 34:1
I will bless the Lord at all times: his praise shall
continually be in my mouth...

"Where the hell is that crash cart!"

Dani's eyes snapped open to Joe's with his loud shout. The grip of his hands on her arms tightened, his gaze intense.

"Wh–what?" Confused, her thoughts became suddenly fuzzy in a complete reversal of her recent bliss fueled clarity. Trying to cope with the abrupt shift in her reality, she fought to make sense of his words, even as her vision began to blur at the edges, and then failed her altogether.

"Joey… I can't see…what's happening?!"

"Charging to three hundred."

"Come on Dani, open those pretty hazel eyes for me." She heard his voice as though from far away.

"Clear!"

Like being pulled backward at mind numbing speed, by an unseen force, she shuddered, her body jerking, as she was snapped back to an old reality.

"BP's rising, ninety over seventy now, Doctor."

Struggling to lift herself out of a deep dark pit,

she slowly regained the feeling in her limbs. Felt a cool sheet beneath her legs and arms, then focused on just her eyelids as she forced them to do her bidding and open.

"There she is. There's my girl." Joe caressed her cheek with a gentle, loving touch as she brought him into hazy focus.

Leaning over her, he was dressed in scrubs and looked older than she remembered. His hair was a very attractive blend of salt and pepper, and he had a few more creases in his forehead, and near his eyes.

"Bless God. I thought I'd lost you all over again for a while there. Just breathe with me baby… in…and out. That's it. Again…in…and out… That's it… Just relax."

"Joe…? How? Wh–what, what happened?" She struggled to speak.

"No, don't try to talk just yet. You're in the hospital. You were lucky. Sky-Med was already on scene when you got shot. Saved your life. You came out of surgery a while ago but went right back into cardiac arrest. I'll explain everything later, for now, just get some rest. Everything's going to be okay now."

He continued to stroke her cheek as she obeyed, and drifted off into a blessedly dreamless sleep…

Chapter 17

Proverbs 17:1
Better is a dry morsel, and quietness therewith, than an house full of sacrifices with strife…

"I can't believe we've both been living, right here in NYC for the last five years and never even crossed paths." Joe sounded his shock three days later as the story of their eerily similar experiences after the New Atlantis bombings began to emerge.

"Well, it is a big city." She tried to sit up in bed, winced and lost her breath for a couple seconds, as the sharp pain in her chest increased.

"Here, let me." He jumped up from the chair at her bedside and tapped on the electronic monitor on the wall above her head. The angle of the bed changed slowly to prop her to a seated position. "Let me adjust your meds too." He pressed a few more buttons. "Is that better?"

"Yeah, thanks." She blew out a slow breath as the pain went back to bearable.

"Anyway, come to think of it, it's understandable. I wasn't really here in New York that much once my practice took off." He retook his seat.

"So many people died that day. Direct impact of the explosions. Some lost to the Atlantic." She sighed. "After the domes started to crack, they evac'ed as many as they could out of the city to different states around the country. Even to Canada I heard. So, in the ensuing chaos they couldn't even begin to keep track of who was who. When I woke up in St. Crispin's NYC they checked whatever records they had, and then told me you were presumed dead." She shrugged off the painful memory. "There was nothing left of our lives in NA, nothing left for me there…without you…and without–" She wondered how to broach the subject of their other tragic loss. How to tell him they'd also lost their child on that horrific day.

"I need to tell you…we…uh…we didn't just lose each other that day. We also lost–"

"Our daughter too–"

Her gaze flew to his.

"–I know. It was in your medical records I requested the day they brought you in here." He reached out and took hold of her hand. Held it in a comforting grasp, as his face became a mask of sorrow, and yet still, such compassion.

"I'm so sorry," she felt the rush of grief return. Wash over and through her. "I should have told you. Maybe if I had…" She shook her head, felt a tear slide down her cheek.

He reached out. Caught it. Stopped its slide as he caressed her face, with a tender touch.

"No," he gave a swift shake of his head, as his eyes glistened with his own unshed tears. "Don't you ever blame yourself. There's nothing that you could have done. Nothing that either of us could ever have done. It was just a tragic thing that happened, one that maybe we'll never be able to understand, this side of heaven. So, don't. This is one of those times we talked about, where you have to just let it go, and let God," he searched her eyes, and gave her hand a quick squeeze, "yeah?"

"Okay…yeah," she nodded.

"So, like I said, with nothing to go back to, I just stayed here. Got the Detective post at the 15th precinct and tried to move on with my life."

"They told me the very same thing about you. After that last big explosion, I lost consciousness. They found me by the sheer grace of God. Shuttled me up to the surface with some of the other critically injured patients, for more specialized treatment. Woke up in a hospital in LA. I caught the first sub down to NA a couple months later as soon as I recovered enough to make the trip. There was no trace of you. Our apartment, so many of our friends…"

She nodded. "I know. All gone."

He rose from the chair, strode over to the windows of her private room, and looked out over the expanse of hospital grounds.

"I moved after that. Joined the hospital staff here. Still searched every record of survivors I could find, for well over a year, hoping against hope I'd find you. It was like the experience of losing my parents all over again, I was just destroyed." He turned away from the window to face her, shook his head, his face a mask of sadness. "After that," he shrugged, "I just buried myself in my work. Did extensive research on cell regeneration, for everything from burn treatments to organ replacements. You know, small stuff, that the defenders couldn't be bothered with. And like the proverbial silver lining, I was able to patent a couple new medical procedures, and then from there I built my practice. Had to do a lot of travelling in those first years, but it was worth it. It really paid off."

"For real." She nodded. "But did you say small stuff? That's an understatement, isn't it? Based on what I read yesterday. Twelve clinics in major cities around the world, with more to come. You're a world-famous doctor now." She smiled at him, feeling emotional.

"Not that famous, if you didn't hear anything about me in five years." He glanced down at his feet, then back at her.

"What can I say," she shrugged, "the New England Journal isn't exactly required reading in the police force."

"No doubt." He chuckled, walked back over to the chair and sat.

"Wow." She shook her head on a smile. "You really did it. Good for you, Joe." She reached out, brushed a few silvery strands off his forehead, and pressed the palm of her hand to the side of his face for a moment. "Just like you always dreamed you would, and I couldn't be prouder of you."

"Thanks Dani. That means…everything to me." His smile was heart-warming.

"So, here we are again." He reached over, picked up her left hand, ran his hand along her knuckles, laced their fingers together, so their wedding rings lined up. "I can't believe you're still wearing this…like me." His voice was deep and soft. His eyes, a sea of so many emotions.

"So…where should we live? My place or yours?" Now he sounded cheery, as he massaged her fingers between both of his hands. "Obviously I'm partial to mine. You'll see. It's a great property, but I could certainly move into yours…ah…if that's what you'd prefer for now, at least till we get situated again–

"What? What is it?" He sounded alarmed, as she pulled her hand back from his grasp as gently as she could. She gripped the excess covers on the bed, crumpled them in her hand.

Her mind froze. Not knowing how to tell him she was scared again, even more than she had been all those years ago. What if seeing him in heaven was some kind of way to prepare her for yet another soul-crushing loss. Just closure because she'd never really let him go. She was straight-up terrified. Only for a different reason this time – this time because she just couldn't survive losing him. Again.

So instead, she chose to shut herself off.

He froze.

Then he swallowed, so hard she swore she could hear the saliva go down the back of his throat.

"Is…is there…someone else?"

"No. Hell no." Her gaze jumped up to his distressed look. "Never that." She gave a vigorous shake of her head, not wanting him to think she could ever replace him. "I haven't even been on a date, far less a date-date, since you di–I mean…since we got separated."

He breathed an audible sigh.

"Okay, then what? Talk to me Dani."

"I just think we need to take a beat and think about this. We've been apart for so long. I have my new life. You have yours. I just don't know if we can–"

"So what? What are you saying…you want a divorce?" He barely got the words out, his gravelly tone breaking on a shuddering note.

"No, not a divorce, but maybe we should stay separated. You said it yourself. Your career has taken off. You're starrin' now, son. Just pimpin' all over the world. Hey!" She tried to lighten the situation with a half laugh as she made a 21st century gang sign with her fingers.

He wasn't in the least amused. In fact, in the moment, he looked angrier than she'd ever seen him.

"Oh no. You don't get to do that." His attractive lips compressed into a tight line. "*You…* don't *get* to blame your opting out of this marriage on me. I'm fully prepared to do whatever it takes to get back to where we left off. Or to start over. Or whatever it will take to make this work. Always have. Always will. If you're going to walk away from us, you damn well better own it."

"Okay…uh…fine." She pushed down her anxiety over the implications of his response. "My career is a number one priority for me right now. I've worked my tail off to make detective. And it wouldn't be fair to you if I don't have enough in the tank to devote to you and the force, at the same time." She shrugged.

"No." He shook his head. "I won't accept that.

You've always been ambitious. It never affected our relationship before. We've always been able to maintain that give and take in our work-life balance, so I refuse to believe we can't make it work again, no matter what."

He got quiet. Looked down at the floor, for long seconds.

"Please…Dani." He raised his gaze, leaned across the bed, grasped both of her arms and this time, looked deep into her eyes. He searched them. "I want my wife back. I need *you*…back, Dani. I've been drowning without you. I can't even explain it. Sinking. In just this bottomless sea of abject, empty loneliness. Please. I need you… My heart. The woman I love…. So I can finally breathe again."

Touched beyond words and measure by his raw, revealing, and potent declaration, she almost wavered. Felt tears fill her eyes.

"And I'm just not so sure I'm her…anymore." Her voice was quiet.

He sighed, raked a hand through his hair then rubbed his chin, as he blinked away the moisture she saw mirrored in his.

"Well, suffice it to say, I don't believe a word of that bull you just spouted." He stood abruptly and pushed back the chair with an angry jerk. It made a loud grating sound on the tile floor, and she inhaled a sharp breath as it jarred her senses.

"I can't force this, so I'll respect your wishes and back off. But just so you know. *This*…isn't over, not by a long shot."

His powerful strides took him across the room in seconds, and he exited the room.

Chapter 18

2 Corinthians 5:18
And all things are of God, who hath reconciled us to
himself by Jesus Christ, and hath given to us the ministry
of reconciliation...

Dani sat up in bed, tapped her watch and started pulling out what she needed. Wright had certainly been true to his word. In addition to what he uploaded yesterday, he'd given her access to everything else she asked for to catch up on her open cases, and pending reports.

"Good Thursday morning! And how's my favorite patient today?"

"Just the same as yesterday, Doc. Ready to get out of here and back to my J.O.B.," she responded without looking up from the screens she had spread out all around her on her hospital bed.

They'd argued back and forth about their marital status, and the way forward, for more than a week after that first confrontation, but without either conceding any ground. At least they both agreed that since their long-standing friendship was too precious to sever, they were intent they would find a way to keep it front and center. So, this kind of civil and pleasant tête-à-tête had become their routine over the last couple days.

"Are those case files again, Detective? Those better not be case files." The deep tone of the reprimand made her glance up as he left the doorway to her hospital room, and approached the bed. "Son of a nut-buster, Dani."

She snorted on a little laugh.

Classic Joe.

She shook her head and kept on working, as he kept on speaking.

"In case you forgot, you've been through a very traumatic event, life-altering surgery and–okay, so that's *seriously* disturbing." His voice got even deeper.

She looked up as he reached out and pulled one of the particularly gory crime scene e-photos across the white sheet, to the edge of the bed.

He turned pale and more than a little green around the gills as he stared at it.

"Really Joe?"

"What?" He looked across at her.

"You cut into people for a living. You literally see them with all their blood and organs and guts and stuff on display, like this, every day."

"No-ooo. No." He gave a vigorous shake of his head. "Not like that, I don't. What I do takes skill, and the use of lasers and precision cutting tools. What'd the guy use? Like a hunting knife?" His head tilted to the side as he shifted the screen a bit.

She shook her head. "A machete. Hacked into her like an animal carcass."

He raised the back of his hand up to his mouth.

Now he really looked like he was going to hurl.

"Unbelievable," she breathed and went back to sorting through her notes.

"What's unbelievable is you. I almost forgot how stubborn you can be sometimes. I said no return to active duty for at least the next month. You're supposed to be on bed rest. Why aren't you resting?"

"Because I've got a half dozen open cases to catch up on–" she pointed to the set of screens on her right side, "–and another four that need reports before I can close them." She waved a hand to her left where he was standing.

"And you're not going to get to return to any of it, if the repairs I did to your heart don't have a chance to heal properly. You're not out of the woods yet." He placed a gentle hand on her shoulder. She looked up and was thrown back five years, as she was drawn in by his striking, gray-blue gaze.

"You could have died, Dani."

That look and his touch, combined with the soft, low tenor of his voice gave her pause. And not just because of the deep note of sadness in his tone, but because she hadn't yet found a way to tell him she believed she actually had died.

"Okay, so what if I pop in here after my shift every day, so you can check me out. How about that?"

"What part of no active duty don't you get? And no, you won't," he snorted. "You know how you get with work. I'd have to keep sending Sky-Med out to the precinct to get you, at all hours of the night."

"Look, there has to be some way that we can

both get what we want here." She got ready to employ some of her best negotiating tactics, but there was no need.

"Well, I suppose I could sign your discharge file on one condition."

"Finally," she sighed and returned to looking down at one of her screens while she waited for him to elaborate.

"You could spend the uh…next week, or two, at my place–"

She looked up abruptly, and met his hesitant gaze.

"–just as good friends. That's all." He held his hands out, palms down, and moved them outward in opposite directions. "I can keep an eye on you while you recover. I've got five bedrooms, a floor with a lab, and a fully outfitted medical facility in case of an emergency. It'll be good for me too…to take some time off from the hospital and my clinics. I've been wanting to get back to my research."

"Uh-huh…" She eyed him for a moment. "Now that's just a change in geography, Doc. I could just as well stay here under house arrest." She scowled. "What's the difference?"

"The difference is, you get to use my state-of-the-art office instead of breaking your neck, bending over a hospital bed, which I *know*, you'll keep doing, no matter what I say. Plus, you get to recuperate while enjoying three restaurant-quality meals–" his voice dropped a few octaves as his brows raised, and his head tilted to the side, "–Every. Single. Day."

Well…the hospital fare she'd had so far did leave a whole hell of a lot to be desired…

"Okay…so *now* you speak-a my language." She flashed him a quick grin.

He smiled slow.

She thought about it for another moment. "And I can leave here today, like right now?"

"Well, no." He shook his head. "I still have to review a couple of your blood test results from yesterday, but provided those are fine, by tomorrow afternoon?" All hesitancy gone, he was back to calm and quiet confidence.

"Okay, you win." She looked down at her files again.

"Not yet…but here's hoping." His voice was a rich, beguiling rumble.

"I see what you did there, yuh know. Think you're so slick huh, don't yuh Doc?" she said without looking up.

She smiled and heard his low laugh, as he exited the room.

Chapter 19

Romans 12:2
And be not conformed to this world: but be ye
transformed by the renewing of your mind, that ye may
prove what is that good, and acceptable, and perfect,
will of God...

As promised, Joe took Dani out of the hospital and to her apartment the very next afternoon, so she could pack some things for her stay over at his place.

They got a bite to eat at a restaurant near where he lived after that, so it was late evening by the time he ushered her into his home.

"Wow…" she tried not to gape. "This place is tight."

"Yeah? You like it?"

"Very much," she nodded. Standing in the stylish entryway she looked around at the ultra-modern décor. "It's a big change from those little apartments we used to rent. That's for sure. Remember the one near your campus?"

"Oh, wow, that takes me back. Practically had to go outside to change my mind." He grinned, as she laughed.

"Good times though." She recalled one in particular, about two weeks after they'd got back from their honeymoon…and involving their kitchen counter…

"Oh yeah, of course. *Great* times." The deep gravel of his tone, plus the look he gave her, suggested he remembered it as well.

He cleared his throat, turned and waved a hand over a screen near the door. "Lock up, set alarm and play oldies, slow-jams."

"Slow-jams? Really? Well, some things never change." She shook her head and smiled as almost immediately, a favorite of theirs from the turn of the century began playing softly in the background.

"What can I say?" He shrugged as a quirky smile crossed his features. "I'm nothing if not consistent."

Hearing a whirring sound and a series of clicks around them, she moved away from the entrance and walked through the living room, or maybe living space was a better reference for it. She wondered if the term room even qualified, given the immense size of it. A fair distance away, she ended up in front of one massive glass wall that was the only barrier between them and the world outside on that side of the house. As she watched, a shimmering energy forcefield slid slowly down cocooning them in luxurious safety. From this angle and in the fading evening light she could see a spacious deck, leading out to a massive infinity pool, sprawling and immaculately manicured grounds and beyond that, an absolutely gorgeous view of the surrounding valley.

"Been here long?" She looked back over her

shoulder, in time to see him deposit her bags on the floor, just at the base of a beautiful wood grain staircase, she assumed led to the bedrooms on the upper floor.

"About two years, although with all the travelling I did, getting the clinics up and running, I barely spent any time here until this year." He began walking across to her.

All the furnishings in the space were tasteful yet lavish, and from what she could tell – hella-expensive. Everywhere she looked, it was fairly evident that he'd done extremely well for himself since he'd left New Atlantis and settled in New York.

"There's something different about you..."

She turned to face him fully. He was leaning against the nearby traditional brick wall that abutted the glass one where she was standing. He crossed his arms over his chest, struck a casual pose that was at odds with the intensity of his gray-blue gaze. "Haven't heard you cuss even once, and you've got…less of your usual edge, maybe? I can't quite put my finger on it yet."

"Five years is a long time, Joe," she shrugged. "I've been through a whole lot in the time since we got separated." She looked away, and then turned back to the amazing view he had of the surrounding city.

"And more so in the last two weeks, I'll bet." She turned, watched as he pushed away from the wall, walked over, his stride confident and unhurried. He drew her gaze up to his with a soft nudge of his forefinger under her chin.

"Yeah, that too." She still didn't know if she felt

ready to share what she'd experienced.

"Don't do that Dani, please?" He ran his hands down her arms with a light touch.

"Do what?"

"Don't shut me out. We promised each other that we'd at least repair our friendship, and I can feel that wall you had between us going right back up again. And it's going to hurt our relationship, whatever it ends up being. Been there and done that. You can cry, kick up a fuss, or go gangster, and break some stuff up in here if you need to. I don't care what it takes, but we are going to work through this, whatever *this* is, together."

Feeling discomfited by his declaration she pulled away from his touch. Left him and his compelling view, and equally compelling words, and made her way across the living space to the very modern and well-outfitted kitchen. She stood at the edge of the floating island that was its focal point.

"Very nice." She ran a hand over the smooth surface, guessing he still loved to cook, when he needed to de-stress from the many demands of his medical profession. He followed her over and stood on the other side of the island.

She looked out towards the living area and then back at him.

"All of it, it's just perfect. Classy, minimalist, manly, and–" she lifted an apron hanging over a nearby stool, "–and so you," she barked out a laugh as she read the front of it.

"Who's your fry-daddy?"

"Uh…how'd that get out here?" He gave a half laugh as he stretched over and snatched it away from her loose grasp and walked to the wall behind him. He waved a hand to open a door, previously invisible, to what looked like a large, airy and wonderfully fragrant pantry. He threw it in. "It's nothing, just a little gag-gift from one of my staff." He leaned back and placed the heels of his hands on either side of him, on the counter near the door, and then tapped his fingers on the cupboard beneath, in rhythm to the music playing.

She inhaled deep, as the door slid closed, and the last delicious smells of chocolate and fresh berries faded, same as all traces of the door.

She grinned at him.

He smiled back.

She licked her lips.

"Oh, no..." He shook his head, straightened up and away from the counter. He took a couple steps towards her, then stopped midway.

"Aww...hell no..." He ran a hand through his hair. "I know that look." He used the same hand as he pointed in the general direction of her nose, as she nodded.

He shook his head again, on a slow smile.

"Oh...hell yes...*fry-daddy*." She lowered her voice to a sensual purr. "That is most definitely going to stick." She laughed with him as he threw his head back and roared.

"Oh, I've missed this." As his laughter faded, he closed the remaining distance between them and drew her into a loose embrace. "I've missed *us*."

The tenor and sincerity of his words drew her gaze up to his smoky gray one.

"Me too." She reached up on her tippy toes,

wrapped her arms around his broad shoulders and hugged him.

Feeling better, she let him go, turned on her heel, sauntered back into the living area and sat down on one of the plush looking sofas.

"I've been praying for days about us, and now, right this minute, I feel like I should tell you something."

The expression on his face turned serious. He propped a hip on one of the high stools near the island. "Go on. I'm listening."

She took a calming breath and then related the short version of her near-death experience.

"So, Zoey… That's her name, huh?"

"Yeah, you know like Joey?" She looked over at him and smiled.

"Yeah, I know." He nodded and returned her smile.

"I dunno, it just made sense to me at the time, when I found out we were expecting. I just knew she'd be a mini version of you."

"I love it."

"Yeah?" She felt her heart expand, as she smiled.

"Yeah." He nodded, his face reflecting her joy.

"So, what do you think? Was that little glimpse I think I had into heaven real? Or was I just hallucinating?"

"I dunno," he shrugged, walked over and took a seat a cushion away. "I will say though that God exists in all times, so when we're around him I think the past, the present and even the future, they all coalesce. The good book says that we were always with God. He knew us and chose us, even before the foundation of the world. So, I believe that as we mark the passage of time here on earth, for those of us who are His faithful, when we close our eyes here, we reopen them again, all of us, in His presence, *and* at the same time – His time."

"Wow… that's so awesome." She felt her heart expand as his assertion resonated with her at a visceral level.

"Whatever the case, whether your experience was real or not, I think He has a way of showing us exactly what we need to see, when we need to see it, to get us back on the right path."

"Well, I can't argue with that." She slid off her shoes, pulled up a bent leg onto the sofa and turned to face him fully. "When I thought you died, and then losing Zoey too." She shook her head. "I was so bitter for so long. Then once I woke up and saw you, I kept thinking that maybe the whole near-death experience was just preparing me for losing you again. For good this time. You know, like some kind of spiritual closure. But then as I prayed, more and more I just kept remembering the love I felt, and what an incredible gift it is, even though it lasted for such a short time. I realize now, I want that for us again." She grasped his hands. "For however long it lasts." She reached over and pulled him into her for a hug. Transferred as much of the love that she was feeling as she could.

They shared a warm smile.
"It's amazing, I feel like a new person now. I really do. I feel… transformed. And it's made me believe again, just like Al said, so much stronger than I ever

did before."

"Al?" he drawled.

"Take it easy Doc," she read his look. "He's just this little old guy I met a while ago. He shared some useful wisdom just when I needed it most."

He nodded.

"So, this heavenly version of me, you haven't said yet what I was like." He pulled off his shoes, pulled up a leg, and mirrored her position facing him.

She looked down at his powerful thigh, let her gaze linger, before she raised it up to his eyes once more.

They widened.

His next inward breath…ragged.

"Oh, you looked good, babe." She touched the tip of her tongue to her upper lip. "I mean, *real*…good," her voice dropped to a low purr.

She shifted forward a bit, till their knees were touching.

"Oh? Really?" His voice was a grating rumble.

"M-hmm…" She gave a slow nod. "That spot near your chin where you got the stitches when we were kids was gone." She brushed a fingertip over the faint scar near his lips, then leaned in and brushed it with a soft kiss. "And those little crinkles in the corners of your eyes and forehead." She put her hands to his cheeks, pulled him forward, and kissed both corners of his eyes, and between them, just above his nose. "Oh, and your hair, it was all thick, long and lush, and back to black.

"But I have to say… I'm really digging this salt and pepper thing you got goin' on now, though." She raked her fingers into his hair, caressing his scalp.

"Oh, it's working for me all right."

"Oh, yeah?"

His eyes were hooded. His breathing shallow, as he captured her gaze with his.

"Show me…"

He leaned in…

She met him halfway.

Held onto his head as he drank from her lips–over and over…urging her sensual surrender, with his kiss.

"Wait…" Breathing heavily, she put a hand to her chest when he finally let them come up for air. "What about my heart?"

"Oh, you're fine," he grated, leaned in and kissed her again. "So…*fine*…" He raked her with a look that melted her bones. "Healthy as a horse…sweet pea." Another kiss, deeper still this time.

She wanted to call him out on his little deception, until he pulled back…

…and quit smiling.

His eyes–smoky gray–knowing and penetrating, searched hers.

His face–a picture of intense and adoring absorption.

How she'd missed that look…

"Playtime's over?" she breathed.

He nodded slow.

"So-ooo freakin' over…" dropped his head, swallowed her gasp, as he slowly devoured her mouth…

…and as he pressed her back into the sofa…

Chapter 20

Mark 1:2
*...Behold, I send my messenger before thy face, which
shall prepare thy way before thee...*

Nearly a week later, just after Joe left the
house, and their bed, for supplies for what he called,
"a feast fit for a second honeymoon", the alert on her
wrist phone went off. It startled her, given the quiet,
stillness of the room.

She looked down to see Detective Wright's
avatar. She tapped it and put it on view screen in front
of her as she leaned back against the pillows.

"Hey Detective." She smiled, happy to see him.

"Well, hey yourself, Monzo." He smiled back.
"We didn't get to talk much the day you asked me
for those case files, and I really wanted to say how
good it was to hear your voice and see that pretty
face." He gave her a wink. "Nice to know you're still
in the land of the living, bless God."

"Amen to that, Detective." She felt his faith-
filled joy, and it was contagious.

"Is this a bad time? Can you talk?"

"Oh no, yeah, I'm glad you called actually." She

got set to grill him about why that creep Charlie Swift had decided to take her out.

"Ok, great. I heard you left the hospital with your husband. I couldn't believe it when I heard he was still alive. An honest to God miracle. I'm so glad you guys found your way back to each other again."

She nodded. "Yeah, for sure. A blessing beyond my wildest dreams."

"Well, good for you."

They shared a smile.

"So, I've been itching to get back out there. What's the latest on my case? Did you guys find out why Swift targeted me?"

"Oh yeah, except it wasn't Swift. We checked and as it turns out, the real guy died like five years ago in the New Atlantis bombings. Go figure. So, I'm thinking, it had to be one of those Verndari shape shifters who shot you."

"No way." She pulled herself upward too quick and immediately regretted it as residual pain from her injury shot through her chest.

"Monzo? You, okay?" His concern was evident in his voice and eyes.

"Oh, nothing that my imminent death won't cure." She let out a laugh even though that hurt too.

"No doubt." He laughed with her. "But seriously, do you want me to get you something, or call somebody?"

"No-ooo," she gave him a hasty and definitive response. "I'm just feeling a little tired, is all."

What she actually felt, was a rising heat, as she recalled how really…enthusiastic…Joe had been the night before…and that morning…

Ooo-Weee…!! He'd just about worn her out. *Damn!*

She took a calming breath.

"I'll be fine. And if Dr. Almonzo even gets a hint, I'm in the slightest pain, he's going to cut off my privileges, and I can't have that. No sir. A sista needs to get her little *freaky-deaky-eaky* on again, after all this time, if you know what I mean?" She thumbed her nose and then giggled.

Wright looked confused for a second, then his eyes opened wide. He turned beet red and cleared his throat. "Say no more, Monzo. You've been watching those old sitcoms again, haven't you?" He barked out a laugh "Well, good for you, for real." His voice was a low rumble as he chuckled.

"So, you didn't say. Why'd the defender choose to become Swift though?" she sobered, anxious to hear more about the case.

"Oh yeah, so that's the missing piece of the puzzle I can't figure out. We couldn't keep him in custody for long, or the one you stunned, because they're not human. I was about to contact the Verndari Ambassador when this defender shows up with credentials up the wazzoo. All totally legit. Turns out he was one of their top statesmen, very highly regarded among them I'm told. It got to the top brass, and they said to hand them over. Said they would deal with the rebel in their own way, with their own brand of justice. He said something to them. Must have been in their language because I've certainly never heard anything like it. After that they got quiet and compliant, and he hauled them out. Don't think I've ever seen a look like that. The one I saw on their faces."

"A look like what?"

"Like pure, unadulterated terror."

"Wow." She held a hand to her chest.

"You're telling me. We've never had to deal with defenders committing crimes before. They've always promoted themselves as saviors of mankind. It's not like we have a judicial system to handle this, so something tells me this is just the beginning. We'll be seeing more doling out of that kind of Verndari-on-Verndari justice."

"Yeah, like a war in hell."

"Well, no, not really. Satan cannot cast out Satan, remember what we read," he quoted from the good book. "And if he did rise up against himself and be divided, he cannot stand."

"Well, you're the expert, Pastor, but seems to me, if the father of lies could do it, maybe it's the beginning of the end for him, when the rest of them start bucking for leadership positions, here on earth, as we speak. Couldn't you just see it, a whole legion of vipers, just snarling and hissing…at each other…and…

"Oh, my God." She moved the hand from her chest to her mouth.

In a series of flashes, it came to her – Svikari saying Verndari were vicious, false gods, and that he was a warrior where he came from, leading other warriors, come to balance the scales. The Hades fire pit in the basement of the International Center. A sudden vivid image of an evil face from her dreams, melting and morphing… shapeshifting. Freak-boy twitching and hissing…

Why hadn't she seen it before? Their takeover of a body wasn't hosting.

It was demonic possession…

"What? What's happened?" Wright looked alarmed.

"We need to talk about something that happened that night I went to Kings Hotel."

"What? Is it about the GQ-holo guy?"

"No," she looked directly into his eyes.

"I think Verndari…are the one third."

"One third of what?"

"Of God's angels… I think…they're the fallen ones."

"Okay, so breadcrumbs dropped and followed like Hansel and Gretel in the forest. No turning back, she's really on board now." Alcindor told Michael as they met somewhere between heaven and earth.

"Yes." Michael nodded. "It's a testament to the wisdom of the Redeemer to have her be the catalyst for the new movement. I strongly suspect she'd have figured it out on her own anyway. Breadcrumbs from me, or not."

"This next phase is going to be about getting the word out, so we need someone who can communicate effectively to work with Marly. But still be on the ground and undercover with Verndari, digging up all their dirt, and passing along whatever info men need to know, when they need to know it.

"You know who we need," Al snapped his fingers and said it like a statement of fact, rather than a question, as soon as he recognized the very same lightbulb got switched on for Michael.

"Yeah, *the original* good news messenger." Michael turned to the left at the very same time he did.

"Gabriel," they both said in unison.

"Ask and ye shall receive, brothers. Already got the word from the big guy."

He materialized on their left. Except he didn't appear to be his normal self.

And he looked really uncomfortable.

"I say, how can you even stand this restrictive form, old bean?" He addressed his query to Michael as he bent his arms at the elbows, then shook them out right down to his fingertips.

"Really?" Al eyed him.

Gabriel looked at him and shook his leg out, as he pulled at an area just below his waist, and grinned.

And Al burst into loud laughter.

Michael crossed his arms over his chest and leaned back in midair like Superman in that movie Al saw Rissa watching recently. "Can't wait to hear the explanation for the accent." He still only managed to look mildly interested.

Meanwhile, Al continued to howl.

"I can't even…with this guy. But yeah, me too. The accent is definitely intriguing. And this next phase is going to be the best one yet. I can already tell." He used the back of his hands to dry his eyes as his laughter faded.

"What? Too much?" Gabriel glanced back and

forth between the two of them. "You know how I just love a British accent," he beamed. "Plus, it goes so well with my undercover persona's name, I just couldn't resist.

"My angelic brothers, allow me to introduce you to – Verndari press liaison Budbringer." He did a neat little bow then raised his left eyebrow.

"Well, don't just stand there, like bumps on a log. Where do we start?"

EPILOGUE

Heads bent in concentration, Dani and Joe both stared at the little piece of plastic on their bathroom vanity.

"Unbelievable…" she sighed in exasperation for like the tenth time. "A hundred years of rapid advancements in science and medicine, and I still gotta pee on a stick, and then wait like a lifetime for the results… What?" She caught Joe's incredulous look. "It's 2126 for Pete's sake." She held up her hands in a gesture of frustration. "This should at least be faster by now. That's all I'm sayin'."

He shook his head rubbed a comforting hand around and around her back as his face split into a wide smile. "Just have a little patience, sweet pea…" he pressed a soft kiss to her lips, "any second now… and…"

"Congratulations you two, you're having fraternal twins!"

"Ha! Ha!" He let out a loud melodious laugh as a 3D image of a tiny smiling doctor in scrubs rose up from the stick's tiny data dot along with bursts of brightly colored blue and pink electronic streamers and confetti. "How's that for scientific advancement! You wouldn't have known that already a hundred years ago, would you? Bless God!" His face was a picture of silly joy. "Are you kidding me?! YES!" He pumped a strong fist into the air. "A boy and a girl! A brother *and* a little sister for Zoey." He roared in pleasure, while she gasped. Looked up at him and then down again for confirmation.

"Aw, hehll no…" She shook her head and waved a disapproving forefinger at the doctor. "Uh-uh. No way. Two kids at once? Nope, I'm not doing that." She crossed her arms over her chest and tried to look stern.

"Oh, hell yes, *we* are!" In contrast, his face lit with unbridled joy as he grinned in triumph.

"We? What do you mean we?" She put her hands on her hips. "I didn't see you signing up for God alone knows how many hours of doubly painful labor, *fry-daddy*!"

"It's gonna be amazing." He grasped her upper arms and turned her to face him. "You'll see. Just picture it. All the shopping for cute little his and hers baby things? Huh?" He twisted her back and forth as he looked directly into her eyes for her response.

"Well…I do like to shop."

"I know. Right?" He nodded. "And then there's all the time off–" he wiggled his eyebrows, "–two babies mean twice the maternity leave. And with my paternity leave, plus I'll take some extra time off from the hospital and my practice. Think about it–a suite for us and the babies for six whole months in one of those luxury astral-clinic, slash resorts, that orbit the moon?"

"Okay, so *now* you speak-a my language." She grinned. She'd been dying to get back to the moon ever since that trip she'd taken years earlier.

"Whatever you want, sweet pea." He growled as he pressed a couple deep kisses to her smile. "Only the very best for my queen."

She laughed out loud then. Let out a little shriek, then jumped on him, as she finally caught his infectious joy. She wrapped her legs around his waist as he twirled her around and around.

And as she gave thanks to her Creator.

For life…for transformational faith, and for love.

Did you read Surrender?

Love is Deborah Lamoreaux's raison d'être.

She lives to immerse her readers in a rich fantasy world where magical faraway places and unwavering fated love all come together to create a delicious, satisfying melting pot of literary distraction.

In her world love is always true, unexpected, undeniable, unconditional and of course… everlasting.

Ms. Lamoreaux only ever comes alive when she's let loose to produce her next work of romantic fiction and each and every time that you journey alongside her, within the pages of one of her creations, she escapes the confines of imagination…
So come, escape with her…